"Are you always proper?"

he whispered close to her ear.

"Aye," she whispered back, licking suddenly dry lips.

"Now there's another pity."

In the dim light, his eyes had narrowed and his expression had changed from the teasing charmer to something more predatory. She tried to turn away, but he pressed closer, and she could feel the warmth of his body from her knees to her chest.

"I must go—" she began as he lowered his head and kissed her.

The kiss was brief, but the feel of it tingled on her lips long after he pulled away.

Neither spoke for several moments, then he gave a rueful smile and said, "You can slap me if you like, mistress, but 'twould be worth it. I've tasted nothing that sweet on the long road to Damascus and back."

Alyce sagged back against the wall, uncertain her knees would hold her....

Dear Reader,

The perfect complement to a hot summer day is a cool drink, some time off your feet and a good romance novel. And we have four terrific stories this month for you to choose from!

We are delighted with the return of Ana Seymour, who has written a wonderfully emotional medieval romance, *Lady of Lyonsbridge,* the sequel to *Lord of Lyonsbridge.* Ana has penned fourteen books for Harlequin Historical, and they just keep getting better! In her latest novel, an heiress, fearing a forced marriage to an abusive man by the new king, hopes to purchase her freedom. Things change, however, when a handsome knight arrives at her castle en route to ransom the true king of England. A forced marriage does ensue—but will it be to the right man?

Judith Stacy brings us a darling new Western, *The Blushing Bride,* about a young lady who travels to a male-dominated logging camp to play matchmaker for a bevy of potential brides—only to find herself unexpectedly drawn to a certain mountain man of her own! And in *Jake's Angel* by newcomer Nicole Foster, an embittered— and wounded—Texas Ranger on the trail of a notorious outlaw winds up in a small New Mexican town and is healed, emotionally and physically, by a beautiful widow with two sons.

And don't miss *Malcolm's Honor,* a medieval romance by Jillian Hart, whom you might remember from her heartwarming Westerns. in this tender tale, a ruthless knight falls in love with the feisty noblewoman he must marry for convenience.

Enjoy! And come back again next month for four more choices of the best in historical romance.

Sincerely,

Tracy Farrell
Senior Editor

Lady of Lyonsbridge

Ana Seymour

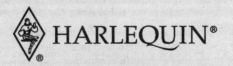 HARLEQUIN®

TORONTO • NEW YORK • LONDON
AMSTERDAM • PARIS • SYDNEY • HAMBURG
STOCKHOLM • ATHENS • TOKYO • MILAN • MADRID
PRAGUE • WARSAW • BUDAPEST • AUCKLAND

ISBN 0-373-29120-5

LADY OF LYONSBRIDGE

Copyright © 2000 by Mary Bracho

Printed in U.S.A.

Please address questions and book requests to:
Harlequin Reader Service
U.S.: 3010 Walden Ave., P.O. Box 1325, Buffalo, NY 14269
Canadian: P.O. Box 609, Fort Erie, Ont. L2A 5X3

For my favorite English Lady…
Joy Hendry
Friend, scholar, professor, tour guide
and tea-maker extraordinaire!

Chapter One

England, 1193

"Whose standard do they fly? Can you make it out, Lettie? Has the baron finally come this time?" Alyce Rose leaned precariously out from the stone casement of her bedchamber on the upper story of Sherborne Castle.

The old servant put a hand on the stiff collar of Alyce's dress and hauled her back inside with surprising strength. "They'll be here soon enough, lass. 'Twill serve no purpose for ye to go tumbling out the window and land at their feet."

Alyce's pretty features screwed into a scowl. "Nothing I can do will serve a purpose—that's the problem." But she let Lettie pull her away from the window and back into her tiny room. Though her father had been dead these past eleven months, she'd not moved to the spacious master's quarters.

In her mind, the sunny chambers at the opposite end of the hall were still filled with the presence of her irascible old sire. It was there she liked to think of him, not cold and buried behind St. Anne's Church beside her mother.

Lettie was watching her, hands on her ample hips. "'Tis not like ye to be so downhearted, Allie luv. The baron's men will think the mistress of Sherborne Castle is a sour-faced puss, indeed."

"They can think me an ugly witch, for all I care. And report as much to my future bridegroom."

Lettie chuckled. "'Tis likely the baron Dunstan was apprised of yer appearance before he convinced Prince John to give ye to him. They say he saved the prince's life and could have had any reward he chose."

Alyce sat gloomily on her narrow pallet. "He's older than my father, Lettie."

The servant sighed. "Aye. I can't help thinking that our true king would never force ye to such a match."

"If Richard were in England, he'd likely pick another just as gruesome. 'Tis an unfair world where a woman can be awarded to the highest bidder, as if she were prime horseflesh."

Outside the window they heard the castle gate cranking open, followed by sounds of men and horses in general confusion. "Shall ye go down to welcome them, milady?" Lettie asked, reverting to the formality she had occasionally adopted since

Lord Sherborne's death. The title still struck Alyce as absurd when coming from the woman who had cared for her for every single day of the twenty years since Alyce's birth.

"Nay, let Alfred see them settled. I'll not march willingly into their hands like a meek little rabbit waiting for the skewer."

"But if the baron is among them, he will expect—"

"If the baron is among them, then I have even less desire to be cooperative," Alyce interrupted. "Mayhap if he thinks his future wife is discourteous and difficult, he'll change his mind and ask the prince for someone else."

Lettie's soft brown eyes were worried. "Allie, they say the man has a fearsome temper. He's been known to beat a stable boy to the ground for not being quick enough to catch his horse."

Alyce shuddered, but her chin went up as she answered, "I'll not be afraid of him, Lettie. My father had no son, but he always said that he was consoled by knowing he'd bred a daughter with the spirit of half a dozen knights."

The old servant shook her head. "Ye've spent yer childhood trying to prove yerself a man, Allie. 'Tis time ye put yer thoughts into being a woman who will marry and bear strong sons."

Alyce turned her face toward the window. "I'll bear no son of Dunstan lineage," she said softly.

Lettie sighed. "I'll go down meself, and tell the

baron that ye've taken sick. But I trow he'll be eager to see ye.''

"Nay, I don't want you to go to them. Let my whereabouts remain a mystery. If the welcome is cold enough, mayhap the guests will not linger. If Dunstan sees nothing but disorder in my household, he'd be a fool to want me for wife.''

''Ye ever were one to tempt the very devil, Allie. Ye've already chased away three different emissaries sent by the baron. I'd not risk further angering the man who is to be yer husband.''

Alyce paid no attention to her nurse's warning. Three times since her father's death men sent by Baron Dunstan had ridden to Sherborne Castle. Three times she had connived and bullied them into leaving. The last group had left three months ago, muttering among themselves about the harridan their lord had chosen to wed. But now that her year of mourning was almost ended, she'd been expecting another visit. And she'd suspected that this time the baron himself would assume the task. He could well be one of the group currently making its way up to the castle gate.

She tilted her head, thinking. ''You may tell Alfred to promise them dinner,'' she told her nurse.

Lettie looked puzzled. ''Naturally—''

''And then tell Alfred to talk to the cook. Has that meat been thrown out to the dogs yet? The mutton that sickened half the castle?''

Lettie's eyes widened in horror. "Ye wouldn't!" she gasped.

Alyce smiled smugly. "I would. 'Tis only proper to offer the baron and his men a hearty stew after their long journey."

Thomas Brand stretched his long legs toward the huge fireplace in the great hall of Sherborne Castle. The structure of the room was reminiscent of his home at Lyonsbridge, but the similarity stopped with the architecture.

His grandmother Ellen would never have left guests to fend for themselves the way the lady of Sherborne had this evening. At Lyonsbridge, dinner with visiting knights would be a festive occasion. Blazing wall sconces would keep the great hall bright as day, and minstrels would be called from the village to entertain the visitors long into the night.

It had been three years since he'd savored the warmth of a Lyonsbridge evening, and it appeared that his stay at Sherborne was not likely to ease the wave of homesickness that had flooded over him since he and his men had once again set foot on English soil.

They'd been to Jerusalem and back, following King Richard on his ill-fated holy war. Now that the cause was lost, they should be returning to nurse their wounds among the warmth of their families. Instead they were obliged to run around

England gathering the ransom to free Richard from the hands of the German emperor, Henry, since Prince John was just as happy to let his brother languish in prison for the rest of his days.

Thomas looked around the dark room, squinting to see if his men had at least found pallets to stretch out and rest along the warm edge of the wall. The fire had burned down to dull embers, and he could only make out shadows in the vast chamber.

"Thomas!"

It was Kenton's voice, whispering, but urgent. Thomas sat straight on the bench, pulling back his feet. "Aye?"

Kenton Hinsdale, his friend and second-in-command, appeared out of the gloom. "The men are sick," he said. His thin face looked gaunt in the shadows.

Thomas frowned. "Sick? What ails them?"

Kenton crouched next to the fire and held his hands out toward the fading warmth. "I don't know. But Harry's been in the yard since dinner, turning his innards inside out, and now three of the others have gone to join him. I feel none too well myself."

"'Tis your stomach, as well?"

"Aye."

Blessed Mary, whatever had possessed him to stop at this wretched excuse for a household? Thomas asked himself grimly. Since they arrived, they'd been spoken to by no one but the doddering old chamberlain, who had ushered them into this cold and dark hall. They'd had no offer of bedding beyond the hard floor, no fuel to build up the fire against the night's chill. And now his men were puking up the ill-conceived meal they'd been given.

Thomas himself had taken none of the dish. His bad humor had left him with little appetite, and, in any event, the stew had not had a savory smell. But his men had been hungry. The rotund Harry, in particular, was never one to turn down a meal.

Thomas rose to his feet. "I'll bear cold and darkness and neglect," he said, "but, by God, I'll not have my men poisoned. I'm going to have an audience with the lady of this household if I have to root her naked from her bed."

Kenton rubbed a hand along his waist. "I'd go with you to seek her, Thomas, but I fear…" He stopped, his face pale.

Thomas waved to him. "Off with you, Kent. I need no help to find the wretch who presides here. Let's just hope that her medicinal skills are sharper than her housekeeping."

Kenton clutched his stomach, then turned and ran toward the door to the bailey.

Alyce delicately picked the last succulent shreds off the capon wing and put the bone on the trencher with a sigh of contentment. Licking the cranberry glaze from her fingers, she grinned at Lettie, who stood watching her in disapproval.

"Yer sainted mother will be a-turning in her tomb, Allie, to think of visitors receiving such treatment at Sherborne Castle."

Alyce wrinkled her nose. "I'd not wonder at finding the shades of both her and my father walking the yard at St. Anne's at the thought of their only daughter being forced to marry such a one as Philip of Dunstan."

Lettie crossed herself and whispered a quick prayer. "At least they'll know ye have a strong man to protect ye. 'Tis not an easy thing for a woman to make her own way through this harsh world."

Alyce swung her feet to the floor and bent to place the trencher next to her bed. "Well, *this* woman would rather face the world by herself than from the bed of someone she doesn't love."

Lettie gave a snort. "This from the girl who has always said that love is for minstrels. Pay no attention to their silly ballads, ye always tell me. In the real world—"

She stopped at the sound of angry pounding on the door. For a moment both women looked startled, then Alyce gave a slow smile. "I suspect one of our visitors has come to ask the recipe for the elegant pottage we gave them."

Lettie gasped, "What will ye do?"

"I'll not have them breaking my door down.

You'll have to open it. But first…'' She stood and snatched off Lettie's plain brown wimple, leaving the servant clutching her bare head in bewilderment. Then she bent to shove the trencher with the remains of her supper underneath her pallet. Jumping into bed, she wrapped the wimple around her head and pulled the blankets up to obscure her face. ''We must tell them that I'm sick as well, so they don't believe 'twas done apurpose.''

''Do you suppose it's Dunstan himself?'' Lettie asked, her voice shaking.

The pounding intensified. Alyce burrowed into her covering. ''It matters little. 'Tis a male, and they're all alike. They think because they're stronger and built for dominion in the act of love, they can rule our very existence.''

Lettie's face turned scarlet at her charge's words, but she had no time for remonstrance as the pounding began to shake the solid timbers of the chamber door.

''Open it, Lettie,'' Alyce said, her voice muffled by her coverings.

The servant crossed the room quickly and threw open the door. The angry man on the other side was indeed strong, Alyce noted from her quickly designed nest. His tunic was short, revealing wool hose that encased well-muscled thighs. Alyce let her gaze move up to his face, which was as well favored as the rest of him. And young. This was not, then, her prospective groom. Dunstan had sent a lackey to fetch his bride. In spite of her bold words, she gave a little sigh of relief.

"Am I addressing the lady of this castle?" the man asked. He sounded angry, but his voice held a note of doubt as he glanced around the room to find her in bed.

Lettie answered for her. "Aye, 'tis the chamber of the lady Alyce, yer lordship, but milady's took desperate sick."

"She's been poisoned then, like the rest of my men?"

Lettie nodded vigorously. "I fear so, milord."

"I'm sorry to hear it." The visitor's expression was concerned and all anger was gone from his tone.

Alyce gave a small smile of triumph underneath the blankets.

"She's been fair doubled over with the cramps since supper, milord." Alyce repressed a giggle to hear her honest old nurse embroidering her lies.

The knight frowned. "It could be serious, then. I came seeking out your lady to ask for some medicines to relieve my men, but if she's stricken herself, perhaps we should find an herbalist. Is there one here at the castle?"

Lettie grew serious at his somber tone and her reply was less assured. "Nay, milord. There be old Maeve over to the village, but there's some that think she's more than half crazed. Most folks hereabouts cure their own."

The big knight gave a sigh of exasperation. "So the chatelaine's sick and the herbalist is crazy. Where would you recommend I seek help for my men, good mistress?"

Lettie glanced at the bundle of covers on the bed, hesitating.

Her voice muffled from the folds of the wimple, Alyce said in a crackly voice, "Old Maeve may be able to help you. 'Twould be the wisest course."

The knight glanced sharply at the bed. "Do you feel yourself recovering, milady?"

Alyce shook her head. The knight took a step into the room and peered more closely, as if trying to get a glimpse of her face, but she kept the blanket pulled tightly around her.

"If the old woman has some powders that will help, I'll obtain some for you as well, Lady Sherborne," he said.

"Very kind," Alyce rasped.

The man paused a moment, as if waiting for her to continue speaking, then said finally, "I'll send someone immediately, or, if everyone else in the place is stricken, I'll go find the crone myself."

He gave a courtly bow that seemed to include Lettie as well as Alyce, then turned and left.

Both women were silent for a moment after he closed the door gently behind him. "Saints preserve us, Allie, did ye see the man?"

Alyce threw off the covers and sat up abruptly. "Of course I saw him."

"Did ye not think him the handsomest knight in all of Christendom? And polite as well, didn't ye think? It makes me feel wicked that we played such a cruel trick on him."

Alyce pulled the wimple from her head and scowled. "I do not consider it polite to batter down the door of a sick, mayhap dying, woman."

"But ye're not sick."

"Nay, but he didn't know that."

"I feel bad, just the same. And now we've sent him off to poor old Maeve. Who knows what he'll find there."

Alyce gave a sniff of indifference. She was not going to admit to Lettie that she was sharing her servant's guilt. The knight had been polite, aye, and more than pleasant to look upon. And it was not the man's fault that he had been chosen to execute the unscrupulous business of Philip Dunstan and Prince John. "If Maeve's having a good day, she'll help him," she said.

"Aye, and if she's having a bad day, he'll probably begin to think us all mad."

"He can add that to his report to Dunstan, then. With luck, he'll become so disgusted that he'll ride back to his master and report that the lady of Sherborne is a sickly hag, that her household is wretched and her people are all lunatics."

* * *

"In truth, Kenton, I don't know whether the powders will help or finish the job that their spoiled stew started."

Thomas and his lieutenant sat with their backs up against the cold stone wall of the great room. It was nearly dawn. Thomas had slept little after his return from the village. As the servant had warned, he'd found Maeve to be a frail old woman who drifted in and out of reality. But she'd given him feverfew and some ground hops, and had promised that together the two powders would purge the fiercest of poisons.

"Most of the men are still sleeping, Thomas," Kenton answered, gesturing to the bodies strewn around them. "They seem to have rid themselves of the problem naturally. Myself, I feel fine this morning."

There was a groan from a dark corner of the room. "Harry?" Thomas asked.

"Aye. He was the worst struck. Mayhap the medicine would be of some benefit to him."

Thomas pulled a pouch from inside his surcoat. "The witch told me to mix it with hot ale."

Kenton began to boost himself wearily to his feet. "I'll see if I can find a serving wench in this place who might know where I can get some."

Thomas pushed his friend back to the floor. "I'll do it, Kent. I'm the healthy one. I'll look for some breakfast for us, as well."

Kenton gave a wobbly shake of his head. "Just

the ale for me, Thomas. I've had enough of Sherborne Castle fare for one visit.''

Thomas gave him a sympathetic grin and went in search of some sign of life in the strange household.

Alyce lay awake for hours after Lettie left. It had become a pattern since her father's death. During the day she could be cheerful and optimistic about her future, but at night she'd lie awake wondering how she could save herself from what seemed an inevitable fate.

It had been less than a month after her father's death, when she was still numb with grief, that the first messenger had arrived from Prince John, informing her that the prince, acting as her liege lord in the absence of King Richard, had bestowed her hand upon his loyal servant, Philip of Dunstan.

When she'd heard the tales of the man who'd been chosen as her bridegroom, the nightmares had begun. But this night it was guilt that kept her tossing restlessly on her small bed. When she finally fell asleep, she dreamed that a number of tall knights, all looking like Dunstan's messenger, were forcing her to eat a wretched pottage of rotten entrails. Then they were dragging her down a long hall toward a dais, where her bridegroom awaited. She awoke with her skin cold and clammy.

It was shortly before dawn. She sat up, staring into the dark, suddenly beset with worry. What if one of the men she had so callously sickened were to die? She rose from her bed and fumbled around in the dark, putting on her clothes. She'd not bother Lettie, nor any of the other servants, but she would quietly slip down to the great hall and make sure that none of the visitors was in dire condition.

If any of them were truly sick, she'd have no choice but to reveal herself and care for them. She had her mother's herb chest, and she'd learned how to use it these past years since her mother had died, when Alyce was only ten.

She had no need of a tallow reed to light her way down to the great hall. She knew Sherborne Castle like the palm of her hand. Quietly, she stepped into the big chamber and paused to listen. All around her she heard the low rumbles of sleeping men, but, she noted with a sigh of relief, there were no sounds of distress.

Surely if anyone was very ill, there would be some sign. The fire would have been built up and men would be awake, caring for the patient.

Moving noiselessly, she crossed the room toward the buttery. She was feeling none too sharp herself this morning, she thought with an ironic grin. Punishment, no doubt, for her wickedness in finishing off half a capon the previous evening while her guests ate rotten food.

The sun was beginning to send slanting rays through the castle windows, but as she entered the buttery, it took Alyce a moment to realize that the

room was illuminated not by the sun but by a blazing wall torch. The torch had evidently been placed
there by the knight of her restless dreams, who was
this moment standing frozen in front of her, his
mug of ale halfway to his lips.

Chapter Two

"My apologies, mistress," he said after a moment. "You startled me." He placed the mug on top of a nearby barrel and gave a slight nod. "I couldn't seem to find anyone about this morning, so I helped myself to some ale."

Alyce stood still for a moment, her mind racing. The knight did not appear to know who she was. She probably looked far too healthy for him to consider that she might be the same Lady Sherborne whom he had seen so ill just a few hours before.

"By all means, serve yourself, sir. 'Twould be milady's wishes. She'd be seeing to it herself, if she was able."

"How does your mistress fare this morning?"

His eyes were unusually dark. They were watching her intently, making her feel as if he could read her every secret. She lowered her gaze. "Milady's much better."

"As are my men."

"Lady Alyce will be glad to hear it." She glanced up at him again, but he was still looking at her with those disturbing eyes. Could he see through her deceit? she wondered.

"Forgive me for staring," he said, as if reading her thoughts. "It's just that you're the first lovely thing I've seen since I arrived here at Sherborne." His voice softened. "Indeed, mistress, I venture to say that you're the loveliest thing I've seen for a good long time."

She felt heat rising in her cheeks. Since her mother's death, her father had chosen to live a quiet life at Sherborne, and she'd had no exposure to the flirtations of the more sophisticated world of the court or the big cities. She wasn't even sure if it was a flirtation that the knight was attempting.

She hesitated a moment, then murmured, "Ah…thank you," and dropped her eyes once again.

"Does such beauty have a name?" he asked, and this time when she looked up he was regarding her with such a charming smile that there was no doubt of its nature.

She hesitated, then said, "Rose. My name is Rose."

"How appropriate." He took a step toward her, seized one of her hands and brought it to his lips. "I'm Thomas, Mistress Rose, most humbly at your service."

Was it her imagination or did the pulse seem to surge through her fingers where his hand touched her? "Thomas...?" she asked.

He paused before he answered, "Thomas...Havilland."

She slipped her fingers out of his grasp and tried to gather her wits, but she could scarcely think for the rushing in her ears. She tried to keep her voice steady, her words logical. "And you say your men have all recovered, Sir Thomas?"

"I believe so, all save Harry Streeter, who may have taken more than his share of the fatal stew last evening," he added with a grin.

"I'm sure my mistress is mortified that Sherborne fare caused such distress."

"Such misadventures happen. 'Tis the fault of no one."

She felt a quick flash of guilt, but mostly she felt unsettled and shaky. He was standing less than a yard distant. She took a step backward, willing her unruly senses to calm themselves. This was absurd, she chided herself. This knight had come to rob her of her independence, to carry her off to a cruel man who would become her husband against her will. The thought brought her strength.

"I trust you will report as much to your master," she said coldly.

"My master?" He sounded surprised.

"Baron Dunstan."

The dark brown eyes blinked in confusion. "I

owe no allegiance to Dunstan, mistress. What would make you think such a thing?''

"Have you not been sent by Prince John to fetch the lady of Sherborne as bride for Baron Dunstan?''

The knight's expression darkened. "I'd clean stable dung before I'd serve as errand boy to Prince John. As for Philip of Dunstan, I beg pardon, mistress, but if your lady is to marry him, then God help her.''

"His name is Thomas Havilland, Lettie, and he's not from Prince John at all. He's simply a knight going around…I don't know…doing whatever knights do.'' Alyce sat on her bed, resting her head on her hands.

Lettie sat beside her and put a comforting arm around her shoulders. "Ye'll just have to tell him the truth, Allie. Ye say he himself called Dunstan a monster. He'll understand that ye were trying to protect yerself. He'll probably admire ye for it.''

"Will he admire that I poisoned his men?''

Lettie was silent for a moment. "I think they've mostly recovered. And he does seem to be a nice man. Ye said he was courtly, Allie.''

Alyce lifted her head. "I said he seemed to be courting me. No doubt for his own male purposes.''

Lettie's eyebrows lifted. "What do ye know about male purposes, Alyce Rose?''

"I know that most men are without scruples."

"Those are yer father's words, lass. He fed ye nonsense about men that was every bit as poisonous as the meat those poor knights ate last night."

Alyce's tone was defensive. "Father always wanted to protect me. If he had known that I'd be sold in matrimony like a prize broodmare, he'd have moved heaven and hell to leave me enough money to pay my tribute to the king and free myself from the burden."

"Aye, lass, that he would, but I still don't hold with the way he soured ye on suitors."

Alyce gave a little sniff. "I'm not interested in suitors, Lettie. I have the life I want."

"But what are ye going to do about this Thomas Havilland, Allie? He'll no doubt guess that he has been tricked when he learns who ye are and realizes that ye were never ill."

Alyce rubbed her nose in frustration. "They're just passing through he said. As soon as his men are recovered, they'll be leaving. It will just be unfortunate that the lady of Sherborne won't recover before they're gone."

"Do ye intend to keep to yer bed?"

Alyce gave a mischievous grin. "Lady Alyce will keep to her bed. However, milady's companion, *Rose,* will serve as hostess to the knights in her place."

"Ah, luv, ye're playing with fire again. If he should find out that ye're deceiving him…"

"I'll be careful. 'Twill be an interesting experiment."

Lettie shook her head. "Ye know nothing about this man, Allie. Who is this Sir Thomas? He could be a brigand. Maybe he comes from Prince John, after all. He might be one of Dunstan's spies trying to learn more about ye. Or he could be—"

Alyce leaned over to give her nurse a hug, then jumped up. "Don't fret so, Lettie. It matters not who they are. They'll be gone soon. But in the meantime, I'm not about to stay cooped up in this tiny room while there are strangers downstairs to bring news of the outside world."

"And handsome strangers at that."

Alyce wrinkled her nose. "I don't care what they look like, Lettie. I just want to hear their tales."

"Still, it doesn't hurt to have a handsome countenance to look upon while ye're listening to the news."

"Aye, it doesn't hurt."

Lettie gave a knowing smile. "Ah, lass, it's the height of injustice that that scoundrel Prince John intends to marry ye to an old man. Ye should be falling in love with a handsome young knight like Sir Thomas."

"I don't intend to fall in love with anyone, Lettie. Women have a hard enough time clinging to their shreds of independence without clouding up their minds with ridiculous notions of romance."

* * *

"I don't believe in romantic love," Alyce declared in a voice somewhat louder than she had intended.

Thomas looked up sharply from his lute. Several of his men had gathered around the big fireplace to listen to their leader sing one of his endless love ballads. It was a strange talent for a warrior as fierce as Thomas Brand, but it had served to keep them entertained many a miserable night on the long road to the Holy Lands and back. They leaned forward, listening for Thomas's reply to the young beauty's cynical declaration.

Thomas let his gaze linger for a moment on their hostess's lovely features. "Love is not to be believed in," he said softly, "it's to be felt."

Her chin went up a notch. "I've never felt it, then."

"Has your mistress?"

For a moment, the young woman looked blank. "The lady Alyce?" she asked.

"Aye. Has she not felt love?"

"Nay." The word was decisive.

Thomas shook his head and resumed idly plucking the strings of his lute. "'Tis a pity, for she's not likely to find it with the husband they've chosen for her."

Unable to resist the chance to satisfy her curiosity, Alyce asked, "Have you met the baron, Sir Thomas? Can you tell me what he's like?"

His fingers tightened on the strings, making a jarring, off-key chord. "He's Prince John's man, and in today's England 'tis not wise to speak against anyone allied to John. But you may tell your mistress that a friend advises her not to go through with this marriage."

A hint of anger flushed her cheeks. "Do you think she would be marrying such a man if she had any choice?

Kenton, who had not taken his eyes off her the entire evening, said, "She's mistress of a sizable estate. Surely she must have some say in her own marriage."

"Not a whit. When a peerage is left to a woman, the king has the right to marry her to whom he pleases."

Kenton and Thomas exchanged a glance. "The *king,*" Kenton repeated slowly. "Not the king's brother."

Alyce sighed. "It appears to matter little who claims the title. My lot is the same. That is, *Lady Alyce's* fate is not her own, no matter who claims sovereignty."

Thomas laid aside his lute. "I'd like to speak with your lady, Mistress Rose. Perhaps I can give her some advice on this matter. Do you think she's recovered enough to see me this evening?"

Alyce jumped to her feet. "Nay. Most assuredly not. She was…" She paused and looked around the room at the men who were watching her, their eyes friendly and admiring. Some were still pale from the effects of their ordeal. "My lady was desperately ill, Sir Thomas. I doubt she'll recover for some days."

His eyes, too, were sympathetic and kind. Once again Alyce felt the flush of guilt. "I wouldn't have her disturbed," he said. "But perhaps I might be permitted to talk with her in her chambers. After all, I did see her there last night. In fact, that's another reason I should see her. I'd like to apologize for my rudeness."

"I believe she was too ill to notice, sir. But I know she'd be mortified to have to receive a visitor in her current condition. I'm afraid 'twould be best if you just give me any message you'd like to relay to her."

Thomas frowned, but he made no further protest.

"You can take her a message from me," Kenton said. When she turned to him, he continued, "You can tell her that I think she has the prettiest waiting woman in all England."

His lieutenant's words deepened Thomas's scowl. "You'll have to forgive my men their boldness and their stares," he told her. "We've been away from home too long."

"I didn't mean to offend, mistress," Kenton said quickly.

Alyce smiled at the handsome young lieutenant. "It would be churlish for a lady to be offended by such a lovely compliment, Sir Kenton."

Thomas looked from Kenton to Alyce, then cleared his throat and said loudly, "Travel abroad makes one forget what extraordinary *flowers* we have blooming here in our own land, Mistress *Rose*." Then he shot Kenton a smile of friendly competition.

Kenton rose to the challenge. "Indeed, the East offers nothing but dry desert growth when compared to the lush garden of English beauty."

Alyce felt as if she had drunk too much mulled ale. She was not used to the company of strange males, much less to being the center of their admiration and rivalry. In some confusion, she stood. "Gentlemen, I've enjoyed the evening, but I should go see if my lady needs me."

Instantly, every one of the knights was on his feet. "I'll escort you," Kenton said quickly.

She looked around the group. "Nay, resume your socializing." She gestured to Thomas's lute. "I'd not interrupt your evening's entertainment. Please continue."

Thomas grinned at her. "Beg pardon, mistress, but it appears the evening's entertainment is about to leave the room."

Alyce couldn't resist smiling. It was no doubt empty raillery, she told herself, but it was heady stuff. Was this what it was like to be at court? No wonder they told tales of the decadent goings-on. Such treatment was likely to make a girl's head turn.

"My absence will not alter your lovely music, Sir Thomas. I pray you continue to play, and I bid you all good-night." Her smile encompassed the entire group, and Kenton was not the only man who looked more than a little smitten.

She started to leave the room, heading toward the stairs to her chambers, but before she could reach the door, Thomas was beside her. He bent toward her and whispered, "Rank has its privileges, Rose. I'll escort you to your mistress's chambers myself."

She noted that he had used her Christian name. Or what he thought was her name.

"*'Tis* my name," she said defensively, then her hand flew to her mouth as she realized she'd spoken aloud.

"I beg your pardon?"

"Ah…you called me Rose."

They'd begun to ascend the narrow stone stairway. He placed a hand at her waist to steady her. "Aye, was it too forward of me?"

"I'm afraid I'm not familiar with the proper conventions, Sir Thomas."

"I'm delighted to hear it," he said with a wicked grin. "They're usually nothing more than a bother, so we'll dispense with them. And you will call me Thomas." His hand slipped a little more firmly around her waist.

The knight's teasing voice and the feel of his body close to hers were creating an unfamiliar melting sensation inside her stomach. She was perplexed to realize that the feeling was not entirely unpleasant.

She tried to move away, but her shoulder scraped the rounded wall of the stairwell. Thomas pulled her toward him once again. ''Let me assist you. A fine escort I'd make if I let you fall down the stairs.''

''There will be light on the floor above,'' she said, and, as they rounded the last turn of the stairs, they could see it reflecting dimly down to them.

Thomas halted and pulled her to a stop on the step beside him. ''Too bad,'' he murmured. ''For I'd begun to enjoy holding you close to me in the dark.''

While it was true that Alyce knew little of court manners, she was virtually certain that it was improper for a gentleman to make such suggestive statements to a lady upon a single day's acquaintance. Still, perversely, his husky words made the blood rush in her head.

Of course, she reminded herself, Sir Thomas did not know that she was a lady. Undoubtedly it was not as great a transgression to talk this way to a mere lady's maid.

She tried to keep her voice light as she quipped, ''Then 'tis fortunate for me that Lady Alyce keeps her castle well illuminated.''

Thomas laughed and relaxed his hold slightly, but still did not let her continue up the remaining few stairs. "Your fortune is my ill fortune. Strange, but last night we stumbled about like blindmen. Where was your ladyship's illumination then?"

"She was ill, remember?"

"Aye. And what about you, Rose? Didn't you taste the disastrous dish?"

"Nay, I..." She paused. "I ate day-old capon. I was trying to be proper and leave the stew for the visitors."

"Are you always proper, Rose?" he whispered close to her ear.

"Aye," she whispered back, licking suddenly dry lips.

"Now there's another pity."

In the dim light she could see that his features had altered. His eyes had narrowed and his expression had changed from the teasing charmer to something more predatory. She tried to turn away from his detaining arm, but the movement only backed her up against the wall. He pressed closer and she could feel the warmth of his body from her knees to her chest.

"I must go—" she began as he lowered his head and kissed her.

The kiss was brief, but the feel of it tingled on her lips long after he pulled away.

Neither spoke for several moments, then he gave a rueful smile and said, "You can slap me if you like, mistress, but 'twould be worth it. I've tasted nothing that sweet on the long road to Damascus and back.''

Alyce sagged back against the wall, uncertain her knees would hold her. ''I suppose one should make allowances for a soldier returning from the wars. You've no doubt seen few women on your journey, and any woman would tempt you.''

''Nay, not just any woman, Rose. I daresay I've resisted temptation more times than you might imagine. But 'twas your loveliness that I could not resist. Do you forgive me?''

His tone was more teasing than contrite. She suspected that Thomas Havilland was confident his kiss would not be considered an insult, particularly not by a humble waiting woman in a small country castle. Yet in spite of the man's arrogance, she found herself smiling back at him. ''Let's just say I shan't mention it to the lady Alyce. That is, if you'll release me now and let me go about my duties.''

He stepped to the opposite side of the stair and gestured toward the floor above. ''Off with you, then, fairest Rose. The brief sample was enough to add delicious flavor to my dreams this night. Perhaps tomorrow I might persuade you to let me taste more deeply of Sherborne's fare. And I do not refer to your stews,'' he added with a rueful chuckle.

Alyce felt the heat rise to her face once again. She was shocked to realize that she found the knight's bold words stimulating. By the saints, what was she thinking? She was acting like the servant of her masquerade rather than the proud lady of Sherborne. She pulled herself straight and met his eyes. "I was remiss in leaving the lady Alyce this evening, but I intend to spend the day at her side tomorrow."

"Then I shall join you," Thomas said, undaunted. "I have some things to say to your mistress about this matter of her matrimony. Richard is still king of England. His brother has no right to impose his authority on her."

"That may be, but how do you suggest she defend herself when Prince John controls England and every nobleman in it?"

"Not every nobleman," Thomas said under his breath. Then he added in a lighter tone, "Lady Sherborne and I could at least discuss the matter. Come, don't argue. Tell your mistress that I'll attend her in her chambers at midmorning. Then, after our talk, I'll convince her to give you the rest of the day free to show me around Sherborne."

Alyce gave an inner groan. "Your men are recovered. I thought you'd be anxious to be on your way."

"Our business can wait another couple of days. I'm not ready to ride away from here just yet."

As unskilled as she was in this matter of courtship, his grin left no doubt about why he was not ready to leave Sherborne. And in truth, she was not anxious for him to leave. It was absurd, but she suddenly realized that she not only wouldn't object to another of Thomas Havilland's kisses, she was actually hoping for one.

Speaking slowly, she answered, "I don't think my mistress will want to receive you when she's not feeling her best, Sir Thomas, but I know she regrets not being a better hostess. I'll ask her to permit me to show you around the estate."

His face brightened. "Excellent. Shall we meet at midmorning, then?"

She nodded, then before she could regret her hasty decision, turned and rushed up the stairs.

All the way down the long hall to her room, she invented justifications for her behavior. After what he had said, her agreement to see him as much as invited him to kiss her again. She would never have entertained such a notion for a moment when her father was alive.

But she was a grown woman now, and though Thomas hadn't come for that purpose, Baron Dunstan's real emissaries would be here soon enough. She had little time left for the careless flirtations that most young people took for granted. And, after all, it wasn't the lady of Sherborne who would kiss the handsome knight tomorrow. It was her maid, Rose.

A little smile played around her lips as she went into her room. She'd had a year of nothing but mourning and hard work. Surely she deserved a little bit of fun. She'd allow herself one more day of this game.

Chapter Three

"I know you didn't bed the maid, Thomas," his lieutenant observed. "You returned to the fireside too quickly last night."

Thomas chuckled. "Perhaps I'm just faster than most."

"Nay." Kenton shook his head firmly. "I've heard enough of your lovemaking prowess from the ladies at court to know that Thomas Brand does not hurry his conquests."

"It's true I prefer to take my time with my pleasures. Battle should be swift. Lovemaking should be lingering."

"So how long do you intend to *linger* at Sherborne while our king rots in the emperor's chains?"

Thomas shot his friend a reproving glance, but his tone was good-natured. "A day or two longer will not harm anything. We've most of the money raised."

"Did you tell your little Rose your real name?"

Thomas frowned. "Nay, I've given her the Havilland alias. I don't think it's safe for it to be known that I'm back in England, even in this backwater castle."

"Which is why the sooner we finish gathering King Richard's ransom and head back to the Continent, the better. If Prince John discovers our mission, he'd try to kill us all."

"I know. I don't intend for anyone to find out."

"Yet you'll risk tarrying for the sake of a pretty face." Kenton's normally sunny expression was gloomy.

"Have some of this venison, Kent. It'll improve your humor." The two of them were seated alone at the long master's table in the great hall. The rest of Thomas's men had already broken their fast and gone out to the yard, taking advantage of the unexpected day's rest to clean their weapons and their equipment.

"I told you," Kenton answered with a frown, "I'd prefer no more meals from Sherborne's larder."

"That's why you're so grumpy—you're hungry. 'Tis not like you to begrudge a friend a day's dalliance. Or is it that you wanted the girl for yourself?"

Kenton lifted his knife and stabbed a piece of meat off the board that sat on the table in front of Thomas. "Nay, she had eyes for none but you.

Anyone could see that. And she's too scrawny for my taste.''

Thomas choked on the bite he'd just put in his mouth. ''Scrawny? The sickness must've damaged your eyesight, my friend. She has curves aplenty in that long, sleek body. I've seldom seen such beauty of face *or* form.''

''She's pretty enough,'' Kenton said, a little too casually.

Thomas stopped chewing and peered at his friend. ''You *did* want her, then.''

Kenton cut off another hunk of meat. ''' Swounds, Thomas, I'm breathing, aren't I?''

Both men were silent for a long moment, chewing the stringy meat. Finally Thomas sighed and said, ''Aye, she's that kind—a woman to make the fire burn in any man on two legs. The devil of it is, she doesn't seem to know it.''

''Nor does she seem much taken by the subject. She turned up her pretty little nose at your love ballads.''

Thomas pushed the trencher away. ''I suspect she's more interested than she's willing to admit.''

Kenton leaned toward him. ''And just how did you come to this conclusion?''

Thomas grinned. ''That, my friend, is none of your business.''

''We've all been sorely deprived these past months,'' Kenton said with a sulky expression. ''If you win the maid, the least you can do is to let us feast on the details.''

Thomas stood up. ''Go groom your horse, Kenton, or oil your armor or douse yourself in the cold water of the castle reservoir. I've a lady to meet.''

''Does your mistress also ride?'' Thomas asked as he pulled his big gray stallion to a stop beside Alyce's mare.

''Aye,'' Alyce answered, withholding a smile. ''She's noted for it hereabouts.''

His eyes sparkled in the rare November sun. ''I daresay she's not as good as her companion Rose.''

''I thank you for the compliment, sir, but everyone says that Lady Alyce is the best horsewoman in all the shire.''

He shook his head. ''People will say anything to curry favor with a noble. She's probably one of those fine ladies who perches on the edge of her saddle and shrieks if the animal goes faster than a walk.''

Alyce let her laughter spill out. She was enjoying herself too much to restrain it. The fine day and the company of a charming knight were proving an intoxicating mixture, and her deception only added to the diversion. For this one blessed day, she decided, she would put aside all thoughts of marriage taxes and brutish bridegrooms and enjoy being pretty and sought after by an eligible young man.

Thomas had not tried to kiss her again. He'd greeted her that morning with a courtly bow, and when she'd suggested a ride, he had been the one to ask if she would be more comfortable in the company of others from the castle. When she'd declared recklessly that she preferred to have him to herself, there had been a brief flare of eagerness in his eyes, but in seconds the expression was carefully banked.

"I don't think the lady Alyce is prone to shrieking," she answered him. "And you can believe me when I tell you that she rides every bit as well as I do."

"Then I'm maligning her, and I must make amends when I finally meet her. Will she join us for supper this evening?"

"Oh, I'm afraid not. This morning she was still quite ill."

Thomas looked around the meadow they'd just crossed. The hardiest of the late fall wildflowers still dotted it with purple and yellow splotches. "What a shame to lie abed on such a day. Shall we gather some flowers to take to her? It seems the least I can do, since the stew that poisoned her was prepared for our benefit."

Alyce shifted uneasily in her saddle. "She'd not want you to fret over it, Sir Thomas. My lady has such a..." she paused a moment to swallow hard

"…such a *sweet* nature that she would be unhappy to think you worried."

"Ah, she sounds like an angel. All the more reason to try to brighten her sickroom." Thomas swung off his horse and held his arms up toward Alyce. "Come, we'll pick some together."

Alyce slid down into them, her sudden, renewed wave of guilt banishing all embarrassment. It had been exhilarating to play the lady's maid, and the disguise had given her a delicious sense of freedom, but she knew it was wicked of her to continue deceiving Thomas.

His hands lingered at her waist for a few moments before he released her and stepped back, saying, "We really should have a basket. Then we could fill your mistress's sickroom with color."

Alyce gave a rueful shake of her head and watched as the big knight began carefully plucking the delicate blossoms. "I thought knights spent their time thrashing each other and slaying dragons," she said. "Your hands are strong and battle scarred, yet last night I watched them playing the lute, and now they pick flowers. You surprise me."

He looked up at her, smiling as he continued his chore. "A true knight must be a man of many talents, Rose. He'll relish a good battle, but should have equal love of art and music. As well as a keen eye for a beautiful maid," he added with a wink.

"And you consider yourself a true knight, Sir Thomas?"

He grinned. "One of the truest."

"I gather modesty is not one of the knightly virtues."

"Aye, but 'tis a minor one. The part about the ladies is much more important."

Alyce laughed. She had never before enjoyed banter such as this with a man. It was fun and oddly stimulating. It made her want to go up on tiptoe and break into a little dance.

Thomas straightened and walked over to her, holding out a number of blossoms. "If you'll not pick, you can at least hold these while I gather more."

"I'm sure you already have enough, Sir Thomas. Lady Alyce's bedchamber is not very big."

Thomas looked at the bunch in his hands for a long moment. Then he said, "You'll still have to hold these."

"Why?" she asked, but took the flowers from him.

"Because I need my hands free to hold *you*," he said. Then he encircled her with his arms and pulled her close up against him. The blossoms crumpled between them. They both laughed as he looked down at them ruefully and observed, "Oh, bother. This won't work, either."

Alyce was embarrassed to admit to herself that she'd been waiting for this moment all day. She'd been unable to get Thomas's brief kiss out of her mind, and, though she knew it was a scandalous desire for a well-bred maiden, she wanted another sample. And she wasn't about to let some fast-wilting flowers stand in her way. "Never mind," she said, bending down to deposit the bouquet on the ground. "They'll be fine right here until we're ready to leave."

Thomas's smile of satisfaction was confirmation that she was acting like a village hussy, but she didn't care as he put his arms around her again and lowered his lips to hers. Unlike the brief kiss of the previous evening, this one was slow and deep. His mouth gently melded with hers, warm and moist, then opened to urge a more ardent joining. For several moments, Alyce lost track of everything that surrounded them. She could no longer smell the dry grass of the meadow or hear the horses' impatient huffing. Her entire world was centered in Thomas's kiss.

He gave a little groan of pleasure as he drew away. Closing his eyes and resting his forehead against hers, he murmured, "By the rood, Rose, I've never in my life tasted anything so sweet."

Her arms had crept around his neck and they tightened at his words. He sounded utterly sincere. Thomas Havilland was obviously a practiced gallant, but there was a note in his declaration that rang true. Of course, the notion was absurd. He had kissed many women. In his eyes, she was just a servant on whom he could practice his skill at flirtation. And he was obviously hungry for a woman after a dreary campaign.

She put the thought into words. "You say that you've been away from home for a long time, Sir Thomas. No doubt the slightest attention from an English maid would seem wondrous to you."

He loosened his hold on her and answered slowly, "Nay. I'll admit I've had few kisses over these past months, but this is something..." His voice trailed off.

His expression was genuinely puzzled, and Alyce was tempted to believe that he had indeed found the kisses as compelling as she had. Unconsciously, she tilted her face, and he accepted the mute offer by kissing her again. This time she didn't know how many minutes transpired before he pulled away with a deep, ragged breath.

"You've bewitched me, Rose. Or have you fed me one of old Maeve's love potions?" When she flushed, he laughed and added, "No matter. I'm not objecting. But you must know 'tis dangerous to incite a man's passions."

Alyce knew no such thing, but his teasing expression did not look the least dangerous, so she smiled back at him. What would a lady's maid say at this juncture? she wondered. Daringly, she tried, "Fie on you, sir, if you think I need a potion to do the job."

His expression changed once again, and this time she did glimpse danger in his hooded gaze and the flare of his nostrils. In one fluid motion he scooped her up into his arms and began walking toward the copse of trees at the far end of the meadow. It was some distance, but he carried her easily, without so much as breathing hard. It was Alyce's chest that was rising and falling in short, panicked breaths.

He reached the trees and gave her a hard, quick kiss. "In truth, I judged Sherborne a modest place when we rode in, sweetheart. I never thought to find such riches here."

Her insides were churning. Though inexperienced, she knew enough to realize that Thomas was intending to move beyond flirtatious kisses. Part of her wanted to let him continue. His kisses had been exciting, and her untutored body wanted to learn what further wizardry he could show her.

He laid her gently on a mound of soft grass at the base of an ash tree and knelt beside her, looking down. His fingers traced the line of her jaw, then his hand moved down to sculpt her breast through the thick cloth of her dress. "Shall I free you of these wrappings?" he asked.

With sudden panic, Alyce brushed aside his hand and sat straight up as if stung by a bee. What had possessed her? The knight might think her a serving wench, but she was not one. She was the lady of Sherborne Castle, in liege to the king of England. Neither her fate nor her body were her own. "I can't do this," she said stiffly.

At first Thomas seemed to think it all part of the game. He took her shoulders and dropped a gentle kiss on her nose. "Don't worry, sweetling," he murmured. "We'll be careful."

She had only the vaguest notion what he meant by those words, but she knew that no amount of care could make it all right for the lady Alyce of Sherborne to lie with a wandering knight. She pushed him back. "Nay, you don't understand. I must return to the castle. Please."

The touch of alarm in her tone seemed to reach him. He pulled his arms away and let them drop to his sides. "I'm sorry, Rose," he said stiffly. "It seemed that you were willing."

She bit her lip and found it still sensitive from his kisses. "Aye," she said miserably. "That is...*nay*. I hold you no blame, Sir Thomas. 'Twas my fault for acting recklessly."

If he was disappointed or angry, it did not show in his expression. He smiled. "Perhaps I went too quickly, sweetling. The fault was not in your actions but in your beauty and sweetness. I didn't mean to press you, but you made me quite lose my head."

She realized that after the bold way she had acted, she should be grateful for his easy acceptance of her change of heart. "Thank you," she said.

He stood and held out his hand. "Come, let's

see if any of our flowers survived, to take back to
your mistress.''

Feeling a little shaky, Alyce accepted his hand
to help her up, but dropped it immediately when
she was on her feet. She was quiet as they made
their way back to the horses. He helped her mount,
then quickly gathered the scattered blossoms and
got on his own horse.

She remained silent on the ride back to the castle, confused at her actions and at how fast things
had progressed between her and Thomas. Didn't
she have enough problems, she asked herself angrily, without losing all vestige of good sense because a handsome knight wooed her with pretty
words?

As they dismounted, he asked about seeing her
at dinner. He seemed a little hurt by her swift
change of mood, but she didn't trust herself enough
to spend more time with him to soothe his feelings.
She gave a vague answer, then handed him the
reins to her mount and bolted for the security of
the castle.

''Thomas, you were the one who said we
shouldn't tarry long at any place lest Dunstan get
wind of our movements. If he and Prince John
learn that we are collecting the ransom for Richard,
they'll have their dogs on us in an instant.''

This time Kenton had recruited assistance in ar-
guing with his leader. Harry the Stout had joined

them at the table, along with a third knight whom the men had dubbed Martin the Reaper. Unlike Harry, Martin's nickname had nothing to do with his appearance. The phrase came from the number of Saladin's legions Martin had mowed down in battle.

"Kenton's right," Martin said, sober in spite of the pitcher of ale he had single-handedly consumed. "'Tis time we leave here before word of our presence spreads. We've already judged this castle too poor to contribute to our cause. By all accounts the lady has not even the money to buy herself free from her marriage duty to the king's choice."

"To Prince John's choice, according to her serving woman," Thomas corrected. "Which happens to be none other than Dunstan himself. Does it seem right to you that we should leave the poor woman to that kind of fate? Haven't we all taken an oath of chivalry to aid damsels in need?"

Harry wiped the grease from his mouth as he threw the leg bone of a rabbit down on the table. "I've no warm feelings toward the lady of Sherborne after our treatment at her hands. She near killed us. I say let Dunstan have her."

"Aye," Martin agreed. "Our duty is to Richard and none other."

Kenton was watching Thomas with a puzzled expression. "'Tis not like you to be so reckless over a pretty face, Thomas. Let's be about our business. When Richard is free, you can come back for this servant wench if you fancy her so.''

Thomas looked around the table at his men. He sympathized with their confusion. In fact, he shared it. He could not explain even to himself why the lady of Sherborne's maid had so captured him. He only knew that when she had not come to join them for supper, the stab of disappointment had been every bit as sharp as the Saracen knife that had nearly taken his life in battle.

Damn Richard for getting himself into yet another muddle, he thought with uncharacteristic churlishness. Thomas knew that his loyalty was to his king, but he simply could not ride away without seeing Rose again.

He stood. ''I can't believe that one more day in this place will jeopardize our mission. The men can use the time to rest and repair their equipment. I feel an obligation to seek an audience with this Lady Alyce, to see that she is not being forced into a match that is abhorrent to her.''

''And if she is?'' Kenton asked.

Thomas shrugged. ''As you say, our mission is clear, but since Dunstan is Richard's enemy, we may be of some service to the lady in the performing of it.''

''So 'tis the lady you wish to see, not her servant?'' Kenton asked without hiding his skepticism.

''I'll see them both,'' Thomas answered. He

looked at each of his men in turn, but none of them spoke. Thomas Brand was normally a mild-mannered fellow and a warm friend, but they'd learned from experience not to oppose him when his expression tightened and his tone turned to steel.

Kenton was brave enough to shake his head in disapproval, but even he remained silent as Thomas strode away toward the stairs to the upper floor.

He had been joking when he'd accused Rose of using one of old Maeve's love potions, but by the time Thomas reached the door of Lady Alyce's bedchamber, he'd begun to wonder if there might be some truth to his charge. The need to see her again was like a fire in his gut.

Light shone around the door, encouragement enough for him to knock. If the lady Alyce was still in her sickbed, perhaps Rose was attending her and would open the door to him. Then he would insist on a few moments of her time to apologize for having upset her out in the meadow that morning.

Unlike the other night, when his anger and worry over his sick men had made him pound until the rafters shook, he tapped lightly. With luck, the mistress would be asleep and Rose would be free to leave with him.

His heart leaped when Rose opened the door.

"Oh!" she said, and her hand flew to her mouth. "I thought it was Lettie."

He gave her his most charming smile. "I hope 'tis not a disappointment. I missed you at the dinner table." When she continued to look upset, he grew more serious. "I need to talk with you, Rose. Please hear me out."

"I…'tis late," she said weakly.

"Aye, but I've little time. My men are anxious to be about their duties, and I'd not leave Sherborne without settling this thing between us."

She was holding the door halfway shut, but he angled himself to look into the room over her shoulder, trying to get a glimpse of the reclusive lady Alyce. To his surprise, the room seemed to be empty. "Where's your mistress?" he asked with a frown.

She relaxed her hold on the door and stepped back to reveal the empty room. "She went to the garderobe, if you must know. But she'll return any minute, and she won't be at all happy to find you here."

He moved toward her, forcing her to take a step backward into the room. "I'll explain that her maid has put a spell on me and drawn me here against my will."

Rose smiled, but still seemed ill at ease. "Please leave, Thomas. I'm sorry, but there can be nothing more between us."

His smile faded. "Our kisses were not one-sided, Rose. I won't believe that you did not feel the same pull as I.''

She gave a stubborn shake of her head. "Nay, I felt nothing.''

She'd never been more beautiful. Up to now he'd seen her with a wimple or with her hair plaited. Tonight it streamed loose to the middle of her back like a river of spun gold. Almost unconsciously, he reached out a hand to stroke it. "You lie, little minx,'' he said gently. "There is something between us, and you feel it as much as I.''

She pulled away from his touch and his hand brushed the cold metal circlet that held the tresses back from her face. His eyes focused on it. "'Tis gold,'' he said, surprised.

Rose plucked the band off her head and threw it on the bed. "Aye, 'tis my lady's. I shouldn't be wearing it.''

A slight tremor in her voice betrayed her. Something was not right, Thomas realized. Was she worried that her mistress would arrive to discover that she was trying on her jewels? The explanation did not satisfy him.

He crossed the room and picked up the abandoned circlet. "Do you think she would be angry with you?''

Her eyes grew wide. "Aye. I'm not to touch her things. She might even have me beaten.''

He cocked his head. "I thought you said that the lady Alyce was sweet?''

Her words tumbled out. "I—I did. She's sweet...*sometimes*. And sometimes she has a terrible temper. The temper is more common when she's sick, and, as you know, Sir Thomas, she's been dreadfully..."

"Sick," he supplied.

"Aye," she ended with a little sigh.

He passed the circlet from one hand to another as if weighing the bauble. "Then I definitely shall stay until she returns, to be sure that you don't get into trouble."

"There's no need. I believe she's ready to retire for the evening—"

"I'm staying," he interrupted, his voice firm. "I'd not miss the chance to meet this mysterious lady who is at the same time both angel and termagant."

She looked up at him, her eyes pleading silently.

"You look distressed," he said gently. "Is there something you'd like to tell me, my fair Rose?" He walked over to her and lifted her chin with his finger so that her gaze could not avoid meeting his. "Or should I say, my fair *Alyce?*"

Chapter Four

Alyce drew in a breath. Thomas's hand held steady at her chin, forcing their gazes to lock.

"It is Alyce, is it not?" he asked again.

She let out the breath with a sigh. "Aye."

He dropped his hold on her chin and stepped back. "And 'twas you I saw that first evening, swaddled in bedclothes?"

She gave a guilty nod.

"Why the masquerade?" He sounded more confused than angry, and Alyce realized that he hadn't yet realized that she'd deceived him about the rotten meat as well.

"I thought you'd come from Prince John, remember? I wasn't anxious to give myself up to my jailers."

"But why didn't you tell me who you were when I explained that I hadn't come from the prince?"

"Well, I—I was unsure. I wanted to find out something about you."

He looked as if he was trying to recollect that first conversation in the buttery. "You were not sick, then?" he asked.

"Only that first evening. I recovered quickly. I've always been one to recover quickly. My father used to say that I had the stomach of a goat. I could eat any old thing…" Her voice trailed off. She knew she'd been speaking too fast, and Thomas's expression was becoming more skeptical.

"No doubt you, like your lovely maid Rose, decided you'd eat day-old capon while you kindly left the stew to us."

She bit her lip and nodded. "Aye, that was it."

"Which was especially generous when you believed we had come to haul you off to a marriage you dreaded." Finally the anger she'd been waiting for flashed in his eyes.

Alyce averted her gaze. "I'm sorry," she whispered.

"You might have killed someone with your childish tricks." His cold tone masked a deeper fury. She sensed that Thomas Havilland could be a forgiving man if the injury was to himself alone, but not when his men were harmed. And suddenly it was important to her that he not think her mean-spirited.

She turned to face him. "You're right. 'Twas

foolish and wrong of me, and if your men hadn't
recovered I would never have forgiven myself.''

He seemed surprised at her forthright admission.
''What possessed you to do such a thing?''

''I was trying to make the point that I'd be a
terrible wife. If Dunstan had been among the delegation, I was hoping he'd decide to look for a
better housekeeper.'' There was a forlorn note to
her final words.

Thomas gave a reluctant smile, and his voice
was more gentle as he observed, ''If he'd caught
a glimpse of you, Alyce Rose, I venture to say that
all the rotten meat in the kingdom would not have
altered his course.''

His kindness was almost harder to bear than the
anger. Tears sprang to her eyes. ''I'm sorry,'' she
said again. ''Your men were kind to me. I wish I
could see the act undone.''

He shook his head. ''I daresay they've eaten
worse on the battlefield and lived to tell the tale.
But just the same, I think we'll keep this as our
secret, if it's all the same to you.''

''Oh, *thank you,* Sir Thomas. I'm in your debt.''

One dark eyebrow went up suggestively. ''Ah,
milady, that may not be the wisest thing to say to
a battle-weary knight when he's alone with you in
your bedchamber.''

His teasing tone told her that she had no cause
for alarm at his words. He made no move to touch
her, and she realized with a pang of regret that he

had no intention of doing so. She was not Rose any longer. She was the lady Alyce. And things could never be as relaxed between them as they had been that morning in the meadow.

"I'm never alone for very long," she said, allowing the regret to creep into her tone. "Lettie will be here shortly to help me prepare for bed."

"Of course," he said, and nodded, his eyes flickering over her briefly. She wondered if he was having the same thought as she. If she were only the servant Rose instead of a nobly born lady, she might be anticipating a very different kind of bedding ritual.

"So it would be best if you left now," she said softly.

"Aye, 'twould be best."

Their eyes met for a long moment, mirroring regret. Then he said, "Sleep well, milady," and turned to leave.

If any of Thomas's men were suspicious about the tainted meat, they didn't show it. By the time Alyce descended to the great hall for breakfast the following morning, they all seemed to know the truth about her identity. In fact, Kenton took a private moment to apologize for any of his comments that, while fine for a serving maid, might not have been appropriate for the lady of the castle.

Their graciousness only deepened Alyce's guilt, but since Thomas appeared to have forgiven her, she vowed to put the matter out of her mind. She was determined, however, to make up for the poor hospitality the knights had received on their arrival. Though she knew that the men had tarried at Sherborne longer than intended, she insisted that they remain for an evening of festivities, now that they all had recovered from their illnesses.

"I shall be offended if you don't agree," she told Kenton with a smile that she was only beginning to understand could turn a fierce knight into a veritable puppy dog.

His reaction did not disappoint her. His eyes wide, he rushed to assure her. "I'd not offend you for the world, milady. The problem is—"

"Then 'tis settled," she interrupted gaily. And so it was decided. She sent Alfred's grandson, Fredrick, to the village for Quentin, the brewer, who was to bring some of his finest ale, as well as the tambour he often used to entertain at fairs.

"On the way back, you can pay old Maeve a visit," she told the young villein. "If she's in her right head today, invite her as well. She can entertain us with her fortune-telling."

Happier than she had been since the death of her father, Alyce spent the day busy with preparations, seeing to it that fresh rushes were strewn in the great hall, and putting Lettie to oversee the cooks. "Have them fix their finest dishes," she told her, then added, "with nothing but freshly caught game. Bring in the stable boys to help with the skinning, if you need extra help.''

"'Tis a wonder Sir Thomas did not skin *ye,* Allie,'' Lettie answered with a shake of her head, but as usual she went along with her young mistress's plans.

By sundown the meal was ready and the brewer had arrived from the village, with a great cask of ale. He'd brought along his cousin, a huge bear of a man adept at picking out melodies on a ridiculously tiny harp.

Alyce was nearly giddy with excitement. Her mother had always been one to make a festive occasion with the slightest excuse. After her death, Sherborne parties were more subdued, and usually attended only by the castle residents themselves, since her father had wanted little contact with the outside world. Nevertheless, Alyce had many fond memories of warm evenings in the great hall. It was almost like having both her parents back to see the room filled with happy people enjoying merry company and good food.

Thomas sat by her side at the head table. His gaze was often on her, warm and admiring, but his manner was much more formal than it had been when he'd thought her a servant. Though it was what she should have expected, it made her a little sad. The smile she'd been wearing all evening dimmed briefly.

He seemed to notice the change at once. Leaning

toward her, he observed in a conspiratorial whisper, "Was the stew left over from St. Swithin's Day or were you able to obtain an even older vintage?"

His teasing voice and wink took the sting from the words. She gave a rueful laugh. "These rabbits were hopping around the meadow this very morning."

Thomas looked at the trencher with a look of mock sorrow. "Ah, noble creatures. They sacrificed themselves to fill the bellies of a band of wandering knights."

"I doubt they were given a choice in the matter," Alyce replied. As she said the words, her smile faded.

Thomas lowered his head to peer into her eyes. "We all must eat, milady. 'Tis the lot of animals to be sacrificed."

"Of animals, aye, and of some females as well." She was silent a long moment, her thoughts suddenly sober. A night of merriment did not change her situation. Soon the real emissaries from Prince John would appear at her gates, and from then on she would have no more control over her life than the rabbits that Thomas's men were devouring.

"Forgive me if I seem to be meddling in your affairs, milady," Thomas said. "But Prince John should have no authority over you. Your liege lord is King Richard."

"Most say that Richard will die of his wounds before the ransom is raised to free him. Then John will be king in his own right."

"There are good people hard at work trying to avoid that calamity, milady," Thomas told her.

The vehemence of his words made her curious. "You sound as if King Richard's welfare is important to you, Sir Thomas. Is it because of your dislike for Prince John?"

She could tell at once that he did not want to discuss the matter. "'Tis you who concerns me, not John. Your father should have seen to it before his death that you were affianced to someone acceptable. Even the king could not have overturned a legal betrothal."

Alyce laid down her knife, her appetite gone. She had no reason to tell this stranger her story, but the words tumbled out. "My mother died ten years ago trying to give my father a son, who died with her. After that, Father seemed to lose interest in everything but taking care of Sherborne Castle. He never looked at another woman, and he had no desire to talk about any kind of a match for me, either."

There was a flicker of sympathy in Thomas's eyes. "If he wanted to devote his life to mourning, that was his choice, but he should not have inflicted his grief on his daughter."

"I think he had convinced himself he was doing what was best for me. He felt that any man who came to sue for my hand was only interested in Sherborne.''

Thomas's mouth dropped open in amazement. ''Was your father a blind man?''

His remark elicited a small smile. ''Twas not my attractiveness he was doubting, it was the nature of his fellow men.''

''I'm sorry. He was wrong to be so cynical. There are many honorable men who would make his daughter a good husband.''

Alyce sighed. ''I don't believe he was always so bitter. As I say, he never really recovered from my mother's death.''

''Twas a true love match, then, and he is now where he no doubt wishes to be, which is with your mother.''

''Aye, and their daughter is alone.''

He smiled gently. ''From what I hear, milady, you are hardly alone. You appear to have a castle full of people who love you. I've heard that your retainers will do anything to protect you, even poison your visitors.''

Alyce glanced around the table to be sure his remark hadn't been overheard. ''I take the blame for that misadventure, Sir Thomas. Please put no fault on my household.''

''You gave the orders, but your people carried them out with a vengeance. That Alfred of yours did not so much as twitch a hair on his face as he served us the fatal dinner. And the old woman who was in your chamber the other night appeared capable of bashing me in the head if I tried to come closer to you in your supposed sickbed.''

Alyce chuckled. ''Alfred and Lettie are true friends. You're right, I have many here.''

Thomas looked around the full hall. Unlike the people in some parts of England, the residents of Sherborne looked happy. Happy and *prosperous.* ''Might your tenants be able to help you raise the tax to pay off Prince John?'' he asked.

She shook her head. ''They've already paid too much. First there were the exorbitant taxes for King Richard to mount his Crusade, then for John to line his pockets.''

Thomas frowned. ''Those are dangerous words in today's England, milady. I trust you don't speak so freely to all your visitors.''

Alyce shrugged, unconcerned. ''You made no secret about your lack of love for Prince John. I doubt you'll head to Westminster to denounce me as a traitor.''

''But I may be Richard's man and take offense at your words.''

''I care little for politics. Like war, 'tis another male invention designed to convince women that we need men to handle our lives.''

''When in reality the fairer sex could do just fine without us?'' Thomas asked, amused.

''Without war and without politics? Aye, I trow the world would be a better place. And we women would be free to run our households and raise our families in peace."

He leaned close again to whisper, "Just how would you have those families, milady, without the, er, *cooperation* of men?"

Embarrassed, she blurted out, "I do know where babies come from, Sir Thomas. But I've never heard that a man needs to be a warrior to produce one, nor a politician."

He leaned back with a hearty laugh. The sound of it made Kenton, who was sitting at a table just below them, turn his head and ask, "Will you not share the joke, Thomas?"

"Please," Alyce begged in a low voice. "'Twas a foolish and brazen remark."

Thomas grinned at her, then answered his lieutenant, "We were talking of rabbits, Kent, and how easily their futures can go awry."

Kenton looked confused at the reply, but smiled and nodded. "Just mind that you don't monopolize all of the lady Alyce's conversation. You're not the only one who's been longing for the sound of a sweet English voice."

Under his breath, Thomas said to Alyce, "You see, I've not revealed your misdeed. My men still think you sweet."

Alyce stood, grateful both for Thomas's discretion and for the interruption in a conversation that would surely have shocked her sainted mother to the core. She smiled down at Kenton. "'Tis Sir

Thomas's voice we should be hearing now that the meal's done. Perhaps he'd favor us with a song.''

''Your musicians are doing fine.'' Kenton waved his hand toward the end of the hall, where the brewer and his cousin had been picking out stately melodies that could barely be heard over the noise of the crowd. ''Our men have heard enough of Thomas's lovesick ditties.''

The look exchanged between Thomas and his lieutenant left no one in doubt that the insult was brotherly.

Alyce hesitated, uncertain. ''Well, then. Perhaps we should try a fortune or two.''

Thomas had risen to his feet beside her. ''Aye. Let's see if we're destined to have luckier futures than the little hares we've just devoured.''

It was nearly half an hour before things were made ready. Servants cleared away the trenchers as some of the men wandered off to refill their flagons of ale, while others sought privacy to relieve themselves of the drink they'd already consumed.

Finally the two master chairs were carried down and placed next to the big fireplace. Old Maeve was ushered into one, while the other remained empty.

Alyce gave a little clap of excitement and asked, ''Who shall be first?''

There was a moment of silence, as none of the knights appeared eager to volunteer. Then old

Maeve spoke, her voice crackly like the rustle of dry leaves. "'Tis your ladyship's future I've come to tell. I saw it that night in the fire." She lifted a bony finger and pointed to Thomas. "The night he came to me."

Alyce suppressed a sudden shiver. She'd thought the fortune-telling would be amusing for the visiting knights, but she'd forgotten that occasionally Maeve's prophecies told of ill fortune as well as good. And the old woman did have the gift. Everyone at Sherborne knew that.

"Aye, the lady Alyce," Kenton exclaimed, and several of the rest of the men chorused their agreement.

Thomas looked at her, questioning. "Are you willing, milady? Or are you afraid of what your seer might foretell?"

Alyce *was* afraid, for some unknown reason. But she was not about to let Thomas Havilland know that. Stiffening her shoulders, she marched over to the chair opposite Maeve and sat down.

"How are you tonight, Maeve?" she asked.

The old woman blinked slowly, as if trying to focus her eyes. "The wolves howl at the moon."

Alyce sighed. Calling old Maeve to the castle had probably not been a good idea. "There are no wolves, Maeve. Perhaps you hear the castle dogs fighting over the scraps."

"'Tis a blood moon," Maeve continued, without appearing to have heard Alyce's words. "It tells of treachery and perhaps even death.'' She closed her eyes. ''Aye, death.''

Alyce straightened in her chair as a second shiver made its way the entire length of her back. With a nervous laugh, she looked up at Thomas, whose expression had grown sober. '''Tis the fortune-teller's business to be dramatic.''

The music from the end of the hall had ceased as more visitors crowded around the fireplace to hear the exchange between the witch and the mistress of the castle. But Maeve appeared to have fallen asleep.

Alyce leaned over and touched her knee. ''Maeve!''

The fortune-teller's eyes opened and focused on Alyce again. ''Don't worry, lass. 'Tis not your death I see. 'Tis a man. He's bathed in the blood of the moon.''

Kenton, standing at Thomas's side, crossed himself and went down on one knee beside Maeve. ''Is it one of us, good mistress? Can you tell us if 'tis one of the knights who've come to visit this place?''

She turned her head and squinted at him. '''Tis the lady of Sherborne's fortune I saw in the fire that night. The blood moon rises for her.''

Alyce had grown pale. Thomas took a step over to her chair and put his hand on her shoulder. ''It's a grim game you favor at Sherborne, Lady Alyce.

Can't you direct your woman to conjure up some pleasanter predictions?''

Several of the crowd nodded in agreement. Still on his knee, Kenton prompted, ''Can you tell us of good fortune, mistress? Of love and children and—''

Maeve interrupted. ''There can be no love for the lady Alyce until the blood moon claims its victim.''

Kenton frowned and turned to Alyce. ''Do you know what she means, milady? Is this a local legend—this blood moon?''

'''Tis but an old woman's ramblings,'' Thomas said, his hand still on Alyce's shoulder.

Alyce had heard no such legend, and agreed with Thomas that the idea sounded fanciful. She would rather hear from Maeve about something more real to her and more imminent. ''Maeve, what more did you see in my future? Can you tell me—will I soon be married against my will?''

Maeve's eyes had once again grown unfocused. ''Aye. Within a twelvemonth you will be betrothed to the king's choice.''

Alyce stiffened. It was the fate she'd been anticipating for this past year, but hearing Maeve confirm it was painful.

''Is it her husband, then?'' Kenton asked. ''Is he the one of the treachery and death?''

But Maeve seemed to have gone into some kind of trance. ''The wolves will howl,'' she said slowly. "The wolves will howl as the blood moon claims its victim."

By now nearly everyone in the room had grown sober at the old woman's eerie tone and grisly words. Maeve was rocking back and forth in her seat and had begun to mutter in some kind of language that no one could understand.

Fredrick, Alfred's grandson, made his way through the crowd. "She's gone into one of her spells, milady," he told Alyce, with a little bow of respect. "She's like to be that way for several hours. I should take her back to the village."

Alyce would have liked to ask for more details about Maeve's predictions, but said, "Aye, take her home, Fredrick. I fear she's grown too old for this kind of entertainment."

Kenton stood, and some of the other knights moved back to allow the young servant to reach Maeve. She continued her mumbling as he half lifted her out of the chair and turned her toward the door. Alyce felt her throat close as tears threatened. She had so looked forward to an evening of merriment. Instead, it had turned into a grim reminder of the fate she would soon face.

She stood and faced her visitors. "I apologize, gentlemen. I thought Maeve could provide amusement. I didn't expect to involve you in such gloomy proceedings."

Once again, Thomas seemed to be reading her

thoughts. "We won't let an old woman's ramblings spoil a merry evening."

Kenton was less convinced. "If 'tis Dunstan's death she foresaw, it will do nothing but make the world a better place."

Thomas shook his head at his friend, then turned to Alyce. "As you yourself said, milady, there are no wolves. And there's no such thing as a blood moon, either."

But the prediction that still rang in Alyce's ears had nothing to do with moons or death. "Mayhap," she said. "But there is such a thing as forced marriage. And if old Maeve is right, I'll be Baron Dunstan's bride before the year is out."

With Maeve's departure, many of the villagers had left. Some of Thomas's men were already seeking places along the wall to lie down for the night.

Alyce tried to keep a smile on her face as she said good-night to the remaining visitors and accepted their thanks for the sumptuous meal.

Kenton and Thomas watched as she crossed the room to the stairs, her head high and her back straight. "If Prince John forces her to marry Dunstan it will be a crime," Kenton said.

Thomas's eyes were hooded. "Another to add to the list he has already committed."

"*Mon dieu,* I would sooner cast my lot with wolves and a blood moon than with a man like

Philip of Dunstan. Such an outrage should be stopped.''

Thomas was silent for a long moment. ''Aye,'' he said slowly. ''It should be stopped.''

Chapter Five

The men moved slowly after their heavy consumption of ale the previous evening. But they were seasoned soldiers and knew that when the orders were given to march, they had to be ready.

Kenton was frowning as he finished checking the tightness of his saddle girth. "You've had wild plans before, Thomas," he told his leader, who was watching the men's preparations with a relaxed stance. "But I dislike this idea."

Thomas crossed his arms over the suede of his tunic. Unlike the others, he was not dressed for riding. "You always were the worrier, Kenton. 'Tis why the good Lord put us together. I can dash ahead as recklessly as I want knowing you're coming along behind to put things to right if I take a misstep or two."

Kenton's frown turned into a reluctant grin. "One of these days I'll not be able to save that foolish neck of yours, as I have nearly half a dozen times these past three years.''

Thomas took a step closer to his lieutenant and clasped his shoulders. ''If you can't save me, then 'twill be because no one can. I'd have no other man as my right arm, and that's the truth.''

Kenton shook off his friend's hands. ''I'll not listen to your palaver. You're merely trying to convince me that this scheme of yours makes sense, when you know 'tis as crazy as that old woman last night.''

''My friend, you know me well enough to understand that I'd not risk the welfare of my men, not to mention of King Richard himself, if I hadn't thought this through.''

Kenton looked directly into Thomas's eyes. ''And you are sure your judgment isn't being clouded by the thought of avenging yourself on Dunstan?''

Thomas smiled. ''If aught is clouding my judgment, 'tis Lady Alyce's sky blue eyes and honey-colored hair.''

Kenton swung up on his horse with a grunt of exasperation. ''I've never known you to turn fool over a woman.''

Thomas looked bemused. ''Nay, 'tis not my style. But she's special, this one.''

''Mayhap when King Richard returns he'll give her to you as a reward for faithful service.''

''What the lady wants is her freedom. If I save

Alyce of Sherborne from one marriage, it would not be in order to force her into another.''

Harry, Martin and the others had already started through the castle gates. Kenton spurred his horse to follow them, but before he got out of earshot he called over his shoulder, '''Twould not be forced if the lady was willing.''

"Do your men often travel without you, Sir Thomas?'' Alyce asked. They were riding again in the same meadow they had visited before, but neither one mentioned those moments in the grove when the knight had almost made love to the serving maid.

"Kenton knows my mind almost better than I do myself. He'll have no problem taking charge for a few days.''

"Take charge of this 'mission' you mention so mysteriously.''

"Aye,'' he answered without elaboration.

Alyce wrinkled her nose. She had tried every which way to discover more about the handsome knight who suddenly seemed to be occupying her every thought, both waking and sleeping. But all he had told her was that he and his men had been away for three years and now had a mission to accomplish before they could return to their homes. She suspected the men had been on Crusade with Richard, though none of them wore the telltale crosses that would proclaim them returning heroes of the holy wars.

"You say you have little love for Prince John. Which must mean that your mission concerns the king."

His horse tossed its head, and Thomas reached down to give it a soothing pat. The day was cloudy and the wind crossing the meadow was brisk and chilling. "I thought I told you it was dangerous to discuss politics."

Alyce looked around at the wide-open stretch of ground. "Do you see any of Prince John's spies lurking behind the gorse bushes, Sir Thomas? I do believe you've spent too much time in court intrigues."

"I've not been to court for many months, Lady Alyce. But then, neither has King Richard."

"So you *are* working for Richard!" she exclaimed in triumph.

Thomas shook his head at her persistence. "If you were truly that minx of a serving maid, Rose, I'd take you to task for badgering me with your queries."

Alyce laughed and pulled her mount to a stop. "But you can't take me to task because I'm the lady of the castle."

Thomas halted beside her. "Aye, you're the lady of the castle," he repeated slowly.

His eyes were suddenly intense, and Alyce felt almost as if he had reached out and stroked her.

Her voice caught as she said lightly, "'Twould be an easier world if I were indeed Rose and not Alyce."

Thomas continued his study of her for a long moment. Finally he gave a rueful smile and said, "Perhaps not. For if you were Rose, I'd not want to leave this meadow without completing what we started here the other day."

"I think Rose would agree with you." The words were not much more than a whisper.

"Then she would be foolhardy, for she would risk much for a few moments' pleasure."

Alyce had little experience of the kind of pleasure he was referring to, but she knew that the mere conversation was creating the same feelings she'd had when Thomas had been kissing her. Involuntarily, she glanced over at the edge of the meadow, to the grove of trees where he had carried her that day. "Rose may have been willing to take the risk."

Thomas shook his head firmly. "It may have been a risk worth taking for a serving maid. But not for a ward of the king."

"Whose body is not her own to give," Alyce finished.

"Aye." There was regret in his eyes and something that Alyce recognized as a more primitive emotion. It made her heart beat even faster.

They remained silent for a long moment. Then Alyce gave herself a little shake and said with a smile, "So it appears we've found another topic as dangerous as politics."

"I'd judge it even more so, milady."

"Nevertheless, we both know what happened here between a knight and a maid. I think 'twould be logical for you to call me Alyce."

Thomas grinned. "I'd be honored, at least when we're in private. Though I'll make it Alyce *Rose*, to remind me of what might have been."

Alyce didn't need any more reminders. Every inch of her body seemed to be reminding her with each pound of her horse's hooves. They'd let their mounts stretch out into a gallop. She eased up a bit to allow Thomas to pull ahead of her, and watched him ride, his back straight, his strong legs keeping the big animal in easy control.

Was this it, then? Was this the infatuation the minstrels lauded? She didn't know. But her hands were sweating and her insides churned, and every time she tried to look around to admire the surrounding countryside, her gaze seemed pulled back to admire the set of his shoulders or the wave of his black hair.

Mon dieu, she thought unhappily. If this was infatuation, she'd rather eat a cartload of the stew she'd fed the Havilland knights.

Thomas had been uncharacteristically slow about acting on his plan to rescue Alyce of Sherborne from her appointment with the devil, or at least with the man who was as close to that cloven-hooved creature as Thomas hoped to see walking the earth.

It had been two days since Kenton and the rest of his men had ridden away, on their way to secretly collect ransom funds from two more loyal supporters of Richard. And still Thomas delayed revealing his plan to Alyce. He told himself that he was just taking the time to think everything through. The plan would require careful timing and perfect execution.

But the truth was, he knew that as soon as they'd finished their business, there would no longer be any excuse for him to remain near her, and he found himself wanting a few more precious hours of her company.

He'd never met a woman quite like her. She had the simple spirit and joy of life common to folks who had the good fortune to be raised in the countryside, away from court intrigues and the pettiness of the city. Yet she was witty and brazen. She traded quips as readily as a jester and debated as deftly as a court lawyer.

Underlying it all was a devastatingly innocent sensuality that kept Thomas tossing at night on his celibate pallet. He was sure that she had no idea of the effect she had on him—or on almost any man who saw her. When he remembered what it was like to kiss those full lips of hers, to feel the fullness of those delectable breasts—

"Did you not hear me, Thomas?" she asked, putting her slender fingers on his sleeve.

He jerked his arm as though burned. "Nay, I…" For the first time since he was a callow lad learning about the delights of the flesh, his cheeks flushed. "I beg your pardon."

She didn't seem to notice anything amiss. They were seated side by side on a bench in the solar, where they had retired after dinner to talk in private, away from the ears of the gossipy servants, who had begun to speculate about the growing friendship between their mistress and the unknown knight.

"I merely asked how long you intended to extend your visit," she said. "I hoped you didn't think I was wanting you to leave. Indeed, I've enjoyed your company immensely these past days."

His smile was tender. "As have I, my little Rose. But the question is fair and deserves an answer."

She looked surprised at his serious tone. "You are welcome in my home as long as you would stay," she assured him.

He stood and reached for her hand. "Will you come with me?" he asked.

Mystified, she took his hand and let him lead her through the lower rooms of the castle and out into the bailey. It was dark, but torches dotted the old stone ramparts, giving them enough light to make their way among the debris of the yard.

"Where are we going?" she asked finally.

"I have to show you something, and it's rather a secret."

"How lovely. I've always liked secrets."

"I guarantee that you'll like this one," he said.

He led her to the small stone shed where the visiting knights had deposited their weapons and gear. Since she'd been in hiding when they arrived, Alyce hadn't paid much attention to what they had carried.

Thomas wiggled one of the torches out of its bracket, then stooped low to enter the shed. "Come on in," he told her.

When she was a girl, Alyce had sometimes hid in this little building, burying herself behind pieces of rusted armor. It had driven Lettie to distraction, but her father had always forgiven her mischief with an indulgent laugh. She hadn't been inside the building in years. It was much smaller than she remembered. What could Thomas possibly want to show her here?

"There," he said, pointing with the torch toward the opposite wall.

Through the gloom she could just make out two leather chests. She did not recognize them as belonging to Sherborne. "Are they yours?" she asked Thomas.

He nodded. "Go on. Open one."

Giving him a questioning glance, she stepped over to the chests, knelt down and opened the larger one. Then she gasped as the flickering light of the torch revealed a mound of glittering gold coins.

She had a sudden cold feeling of dread at the pit of her stomach. *Ye know nothing about this man,* Lettie had said. *He could be a brigand.* Alyce had chosen to ignore the warning. She'd been too exhilarated by all the feelings his presence seemed to produce in her.

She looked up at him and gulped, "Is it stolen?"

Thomas barked out a laugh. "Nay, my adventure-seeking Rose. I'm sorry to disappoint you, but there's not an ill-gotten farthing in the lot."

Alyce sagged in relief. "Then what...?"

Thomas's expression grew serious. "Here's where the secret part comes in. This is money raised to ransom Richard from the emperor. There are some in this country who would be very happy to see that it never reaches its destination."

"Like Prince John," Alyce murmured.

"Aye, and Philip of Dunstan."

"I'm pleased that you trust me, Thomas. But if the money is such a secret, I'm wondering why you've showed it to me. And why it's sitting here in a horse shed instead of somewhere under guard."

"A guard would only announce the presence of something important, which would raise people's curiosity. If you treat something as if it's not im-

portant, no one will pay any attention to it. It's a
trick we learned from the Arabs.''

"So you *were* on Crusade with Richard?"

"Aye."

"What about my other question?"

"Why am I showing it to you?"

"Aye."

Holding the torch aloft, he walked over and
knelt beside her. With his free hand he sifted
through the coins. "It's pretty in a way, isn't it?
The glitter of gold coin."

"Not as pretty as a field of bluebells on a spring
day," she retorted.

Thomas laughed. "Ah, Alyce Rose, I swear you
are a female without price. But since the law has
seen fit to bestow one on you, we have no recourse
left but to pay it."

Alyce looked puzzled. "You refer to the marriage tax?"

Thomas picked up a fistful of coins, then let
them clink one by one back onto the pile. "On
second thought, you're right. There's little of
beauty about money. But it has a purpose. In some
cases, more than one purpose. The purpose of this
money, for example, is to buy the freedom of our
rightful king."

"Aye, King Richard—"

He let the last coin fall and held up his hand.
"But first, it's going to buy the freedom of a certain beautiful lady."

Her eyes widened. ''I don't understand.''

He shut the lid of the chest. ''There's enough here to pay the tax Prince John is demanding five times over.''

''I can see that. But I'd not take money that is destined for Richard. The king's fate is more important than mine.''

''The good folks of Sherborne might debate that, but it doesn't matter. The money will serve both goals. We're merely going to borrow it for a while to free you from this damnable marriage John's trying to foist upon you.''

''But to do that you'd have to give the money to Prince John or, rather, to the noble who is his representative in this affair.''

''And that man is Baron Dunstan,'' Thomas confirmed.

Alyce nodded.

''Aye. We'll deliver this gold right into the hands of Philip of Dunstan,'' Thomas said.

''But then...'' Alyce hesitated ''...how would you get it back?''

Thomas grinned and, for the first time since he had learned her true identity, leaned over and kissed her. ''That will be the fun part, Alyce Rose. We'll steal it back.''

''I still don't understand why they would do this for me, Lettie,'' Alyce said as her maid brushed her long hair in preparation for bed.

"Ye will insist on riding without yer cap, Allie," the older woman complained, tugging the brush through a nasty tangle.

"He doesn't even know me. Why would he put himself at risk with Prince John?"

Lettie stopped brushing and put a hand on her hip. "Did ye ever stop to think that he's just being a decent human being? An honorable knight who saw a maiden in distress and decided to help?"

Alyce shook her head. "Nay. I may have grown up young and innocent, tucked away here at Sherborne, but my father taught me well. Men are ever after their own interests."

"Sometimes I think yer father did ye no favor by making ye so skittish about men, Allie."

"His teachings have served me well. The men who have come here since Father's death—"

"—were horrid and rude. But look at the nature of the man they represented. Not all men are like Baron Dunstan."

"They camped here, eating my food and drinking my wine, with my father not cold in his grave, telling me that they would take over the management of Sherborne. That the baron wanted to relieve me of the burden."

"'Twas callous of the baron," Lettie agreed. "No one could blame ye for what ye did."

Alyce smiled a little, remembering. The first group had been easily dispatched, not caring to stay around when confronted by her village friends, the brewer and his cousin, who together weighed a total of nearly fifty stone.

They'd been succeeded by a second delegation, led by an officious looking weasel of a man who'd declared that he'd been sent by the baron to be her new accountant. The poor man had fled in abject panic, no doubt well aware of the baron's reputation for wrath, when Alyce had pretended that she wanted to seduce him.

"We did manage to take care of them all, didn't we?" she asked Lettie with a grin.

"At the cost of ten years' growth," the nurse answered, pointing to her gray head. "With that last group, when ye were teetering on the edge of the castle parapet threatening to jump, my heart nearly stopped."

"By then the baron knew enough to send seasoned soldiers. I couldn't scare them off. If I hadn't climbed up on the wall, I do believe they would have lasted us out until the year was up and they could take me to Dunstan."

Lettie nodded. "Ye may be right, Allie. They were tough, that last bunch. I think yer bridegroom sent them to keep an eye on ye."

"So that the rich prize wouldn't slip from his fingers," Alyce said with disgust.

"No doubt, luv."

Alyce giggled. "I'd give a good deal to see Baron Dunstan's face when they tell him that I've paid the tax and will not be his wife after all."

Lettie smiled and resumed brushing her charge's long locks. "Ye see, it scarcely matters *why* Sir Thomas is willing to help ye. The important thing is that we'll be free."

"Oh, I have no intention of turning down his offer. I just realize that since he's a man, he's doing it for his own reasons."

Lettie's mouth dropped open. She leaned toward Alyce and asked in an embarrassed voice, "Allie, ye don't think the man has, um, *designs* on ye? I mean, he hasn't tried to be forward with ye in any way?" She blushed. "Ye've not had a mother, lass, and ye probably don't even know what I'm talking about, do ye?"

Alyce gave her nurse an indulgent smile. If her knowledge of what went on between men and women had been based solely on what she had gleaned from Lettie, she'd still believe that babies arrived floating down the millstream on Witches' Night. "I know what you're talking about, Lettie. And the answer is, I don't know if Sir Thomas has *designs* on me."

As she said the words she felt the same pleasant tingling she'd had that afternoon on the meadow. If Lettie's "designs" were the reason Thomas was helping her, Alyce wasn't at all sure that she found the idea disagreeable.

"Would a little lovemaking be enough to make a man do something as reckless as he's proposing?'' she asked, then regretted the question as she saw the shock on her old nurse's face.

''Entire wars have been fought over such matters, Allie. 'Tis a dangerous business. And if Sir Thomas has any such thing in mind, ye'd better set him straight at once.''

Alyce pushed the brush away. ''That's enough for tonight, Lettie. I'm tired.''

Lettie bent her head to look into Alyce's face. ''I mean it, lass. Promise me ye'll take care not to do anything foolish.''

Alyce jumped back on the bed and burrowed into the covers, hugging them around her as if they were Thomas Havilland's wool-clad arms. ''Ah, Lettie,'' she said with an impish grin. ''When have you ever known me to do anything foolish?''

Chapter Six

"Please don't argue with me, Thomas. This is my life and my marriage, and I *am* going with you."

She'd confronted him at breakfast before he'd even taken a sip of ale to wash the mustiness of night from his mouth. Thomas groaned. "By rights, the money should be delivered by a messenger. I'm riding to Dunstan Castle with it myself because I'll be meeting my men there. But none of us will go inside. I've no desire to confront Dunstan in his own lair."

"What do you intend to do? Leave the gold at the castle gate and run like children playing a prank?"

"No," he said with exaggerated patience. "We'll be sending it with a messenger, but he's not one of my men."

"Who will it be, then? And why can't I ride to

the castle with him? I'd at least like to see this
bridegroom I'm escaping from.''

Thomas couldn't decide whether to be angry or
amused. Alyce's combination of daring and naiveté
was part of her charm, but he knew that she had
no idea what a dangerous game she was trying to
play. "I can't let you come, Alyce. Once Dunstan
has the money for Prince John, my men and I will
have to finish the deed and steal it back for Richard. I won't have time to be escorting you around
the countryside. I'm sorry.''

Alyce chewed absently at a hard piece of bread.
"Lettie and Alfred could ride with us. After we've
delivered the money, they can escort me back here.
You won't have to concern yourself.''

He bit back an expletive. "Lettie and Alfred?
An ancient house servant and a nursemaid? Jesu,
Alyce, you are out of your mind.''

"It's my life, Thomas,'' she said again. "I want
to go with you.'' Then she did that little thing of
wrinkling her perfectly formed nose, and Thomas
felt the anger draining out of him. By the saints,
she'd besotted him, he berated himself. He
couldn't explain it, but he was perilously close to
forgetting all good sense and giving in to whatever
she asked of him. He'd always heard that love
could turn the hardest man into a fool, but he'd
never experienced the truth of the statement until
now.

He shook his head, hardly believing his own

words as he told her, "If you want to take three or four of your men—castle guards, not your servant and your chamberlain—you may ride with me as far as the castle. But you'll not have contact with Dunstan in any way. When the money is delivered, you have to agree to turn around and ride straight back here. We can't be entirely sure what Dunstan's reaction will be when he discovers that he's lost you."

"Fine," she said quickly. "I agree."

Alyce's smile was bright and held just enough triumph to make Thomas regret his capitulation. "You'll do everything I say and not try any tricks," he warned.

"Aye, Thomas. I'll be just like a good little soldier."

No longer hungry, he pushed away the trencher of breakfast and took a great swallow of ale instead. "It's two days to Dunstan Castle. We'll have to sleep out on the road tonight. I don't want to risk stopping at an inn and having Dunstan get wind of our errand."

Her eyes sparkled. "I'd like that. It will make it more of an adventure."

Thomas shook his head. Aye, an adventure. It was beginning to feel as if he'd been on one long adventure ever since he'd first set eyes on the lady of Sherborne. "Pick your men, then. The best and the bravest. And make yourself ready. We ride tomorrow at dawn."

* * *

The Sherborne ancestor who had built Sherborne Castle more than a hundred years before, at the height of the problems between the Normans and the Saxons, had provided the stone walls, ramparts and moat of a true fortress. However, the estate was far from any city of note and off the main thoroughfares that crisscrossed the country. The residents of the small but imposing structure had never had to mount a defense. There were few visitors, friendly or otherwise.

When Thomas had asked Alyce to bring three members of her castle guard, she hadn't bothered to explain that the position was not one that would guarantee what Thomas would call "warriors."

She introduced them to him one by one. "This is Fredrick, grandson of my chamberlain, Alfred. And his cousin Hugh. And Hugh's cousin, Guelph."

Thomas surveyed the trio with misgiving. "Don't you men have swords?" he asked them.

There was a general shaking of heads. "Bows, then?"

Fredrick spoke for the group. "Oh, aye, sir. We'll nab ye a rabbit at half a furlong. Guelph's the best shot in the shire. I'm next. Hugh doesn't see from his left eye, so he's off the mark at times, but he's strong."

Thomas sighed. "If there's trouble, it will be

more than rabbits you'll be asked to shoot, lads. Do you understand that?''

The three young men nodded solemnly. Thomas looked over at Alyce. She was dressed for the ride in a leather kirtle and jacket, but the thick garments in no way disguised the allure of her female figure. ''I must be mad to allow you to go,'' he told her.

She made a little face. ''You're not *allowing* me to do anything, Sir Thomas. I'm mistress here, remember. And it's my choice to accompany you on a mission that is of such import to my future.''

Fredrick, a likable, eager lad of no more than twenty years, bobbed his head and added his own words on his mistress's behalf. ''Ye might as well stop trying to fight it, Sir Thomas. Lady Alyce has always been one to have things her way.'' He sent a smile of apology to Alyce. ''Beggin' yer pardon, milady. 'Tis not meant as criticism. The people of Sherborne would not have things any different.''

Alyce laughed. ''If you're worried that you'll hurt my feelings by telling Sir Thomas that I've been spoiled these past twenty years, have no fear. 'Tis nothing but the truth. I've been greatly blessed to be raised in this place, among so many kind friends.'' Her fond smile included all three of the chosen guards. ''And I want nothing more than to put all this wedding nonsense behind me so that I can return to Sherborne and live out the rest of my life in the same privileged fashion.''

''Amen to that, milady,'' Fredrick agreed.

Still surveying the three men with a doubtful expression, Thomas asked them, "Do you have mounts?"

"Aye, sir. Hugh rides in between the two of us, since he only sees on the one side."

Thomas rolled his eyes and turned to Alyce. "You are determined to do this thing?"

Her eyes dancing with excitement, she gave a firm nod.

With a shrug of resignation, Thomas started toward his horse without waiting to help Alyce to mount. "Come on, then," he said. "We've a hard ride ahead."

The adventure did not seem quite as exciting to Alyce by the time Thomas pulled off the road at a thick stretch of forest and proclaimed that they could finally stop for the night. They'd been riding almost nonstop since just after dawn, and Alyce felt as if every bone in her body had been jarred into an unaccustomed position.

It was already dark, but a nearly full moon had risen in the late afternoon to keep the landscape illuminated.

This time Thomas came over to help her dismount. "I'll have to admit it, Alyce Rose. You are one tough little lady."

She slid into his arms. He caught her, then set her on the ground and released her immediately without comment. "I told you that first day that

Alyce could ride every bit as well as Rose,'' she said with a tired smile.

"I had no doubts about the riding. 'Tis the stamina that's impressed me. I expected you to head back to Sherborne by midday."

Alyce frowned. "Did you now? And is that why you kept pushing us to ride hour after hour when I'd understood that Dunstan is an *easy* two days' ride from Sherborne?"

He gave a rueful nod of admission.

"You were trying to get rid of me?"

Thomas reached out a finger to wipe a smudge of dirt off her cheek. "Ah, my fair Alyce, the last thing I want is to be rid of you. But I'm not thrilled to have you with me on this particular journey. You don't know what kind of man Dunstan is."

She tossed her head. "Well, your plan didn't succeed. I'm still here. And now I trust we can sleep late in the morning, since we'll be only a *short* day's ride from the castle."

"Sleep as late as you like, milady, if the noise of the jackdaws cackling doesn't awaken you. Have you ever slept outside before?"

She shook her head. Fredrick and the two cousins had taken all the horses to tie them up for the night. She stood alone with Thomas. Her knees were so shaky from the long hours of riding that she was afraid to move, but she would not admit it.

He saved her pride by taking her arm in a

steadying grasp. "Allow me to escort you to your quarters, milady," he said with mock formality.

She gave him a grateful smile. Trying not to look wobbly, she let him lead her down a gentle slope to a small clearing well away from the road. Alyce looked around curiously. "Do we just drop down on the dirt and go to sleep?"

He smiled. "I've been known to do exactly that when on the march, but no. We'll fashion you a bed of sorts. After we pick a place, I'll fetch some blankets from the horses."

They found a spot that looked more or less level, and Alyce sank gratefully to the ground to wait as Thomas made his way back to the horses. She'd almost fallen asleep sitting up when he returned, carrying an armload of blankets.

"These should keep you comfortable and warm," he said, dropping the pile in front of her.

She looked behind him. "Where are the others?"

"They'll bed down at three different points along the road. If anyone comes, they should wake and be able to alert the others of any possible danger."

"No one ever travels these back roads at night."

"Aye, that's precisely the problem. If anyone should come along, it's probably someone up to mischief."

All at once Alyce realized that for the first time in her life, she was about to spend the night with a strange man, alone and unchaperoned. She looked up at his big form looming above her in the moonlight. She wasn't afraid of him, but she was uneasy. Suddenly it became clear why Lettie had been so opposed to this journey.

Her mouth dry, she stood and began to shake out the blankets. "Shall I make up my bed right here?" she asked him.

"Aye. 'Tis as good a place as any."

She tossed one of the blankets over the grass, then, with a moment of hesitation, offered him the next. "Where will your bed be?"

She'd tried to make her voice sound casual, but she had the feeling that he could sense her nervousness. "I'll not need a bed this night. I intend to sit up and keep watch over a certain little Rose."

"Surely not! You agreed that there are few travelers here. I can't believe you need to stay awake."

"I don't mind. In battle you get used to going many days with little sleep. And I'll be having a much more pleasant sight to contemplate during my night's vigil than I ever did on the Crusades."

She blushed. Somehow the thought of him watching her as she lay sleeping seemed incredibly intimate. "If I hadn't insisted on coming, you'd have been able to sleep tonight."

"Aye, but I'd not have had your sweet company." His voice held no hint of reproach.

She pulled the blankets around her and lay back with a sigh. "You are a special man, Thomas of

Havilland. You've been forgiving and patient and honest with me in every way.''

It was too dark to see the small frown that came over his face at her words. ''Sleep now, Alyce Rose. Dawn will be upon us before you know it.''

The ground was cold and hard, and Alyce thought that it would be hours before she'd drift into an exhausted sleep, but he repeated the words, softly, with his mellow balladeer's voice. ''Go to sleep, fair Rose...'' And before he had finished saying her name, she had dozed off.

Thomas laid his head against the hard trunk of a tree. He had no desire to sleep. Long days on the march had taught him to put his body into a kind of resting state as he swayed along to his horse's gait. It felt good to be sitting still for a while, but he didn't feel noticeably tired.

Even if he had been tired, he reckoned that he might be too restless for sleep. His thoughts were racing—first to the task ahead of them tomorrow and then back to the woman who lay in peaceful slumber not two yards distant.

Her last words to him had been touchingly trusting, and it was a trust he did not fully deserve. Though he was not trying to deceive her or take advantage of her as had the men who'd visited her since her father's death, he *had* lied to her. He hadn't told her about his history with Dunstan. He hadn't even told her his real name.

Of course, he reminded himself, she'd lied to him about *her* name, too. So perhaps they were even. When he'd accomplished his mission and freed Richard, he would come back to Sherborne and tell her of Lyonsbridge. He'd tell her of his Saxon grandfather, Connor, who had forged a peace between Norman and Saxon at the great estate many years ago by winning the love of the Norman beauty, Ellen of Wakefield.

It had been Connor who had taught Thomas to play the lute. Big, bold Connor, who had won many battles by his brawn, but had made his most important conquest with his music, his charm and, ultimately, his love. Connor and Ellen had ruled over a peaceful Lyonsbridge for many years, their love a fierce bond that would allow no Norman-Saxon rivalry to threaten their happiness.

Thomas felt a pang of homesickness. He missed his grandparents. He believed them to be well, since he had heard no news to the contrary. But they had both passed fourscore years. He knew he didn't have too many more years to enjoy their company. That was one of the most pressing reasons he wanted to be done with this mission. He wanted to resume a peaceful life back at Lyonsbridge. More and more he'd come to realize that the life he envisioned there for himself now included a troublesome blue-eyed imp named Alyce Rose.

What would his grandparents think of her? he

wondered. Grandfather Connor would say that she was beautiful, much like his Ellen. And Grandmother Ellen would say that she was impudent and independent and stubborn, very much like herself.

He could almost see them, nodding approval and sharing that special gaze they always seemed to have just for each other. Suddenly he wanted to wake Alyce up and tell her all about them and all about Lyonsbridge. He wanted to tell her his real name and explain how he'd had to work in secret so that Prince John would not discover their progress in freeing his brother.

He let his head fall back against the tree with a thump. Of course, he could do no such thing. It would not only put his men at risk, but Alyce, as well. If Richard never returned to England, everyone who worked on his behalf or who had knowledge of those efforts could be accused of treason.

No, Thomas would have to continue to keep his secrets from her for a while longer. But when the ransom was paid...when Richard returned... He looked over at her sleeping form. She'd turned, and he could see her face in the moonlight.

No, we've not been honest with each other, he told her silently. But soon, my fair Alyce Rose, there will be no more need for secrets between us.

The dreams had come again. The guards were dragging her down the aisle of a church toward a giant of a man, clad in silver armor that hid his face. As she approached, she realized that the altar at the front of the church had been replaced by a huge yellow moon, and it was dripping with drops of dark red blood...

She fought against the arms holding her, thrashing about with all her strength.

"Sweetheart, calm yourself."

Gradually she recognized Thomas's urgent whisper. She stopped struggling. It was no hostile guard holding her, but Thomas himself. Her heartbeat slowed, and she opened her eyes to find his face inches above hers, his eyes worried.

"It's just a dream," she said, her voice hoarse. "They come every now and then."

He pulled her more firmly into his arms. "What dreams are these, my little Rose?"

She shook her head. "'Tis nothing. I never had a bad dream in my life while my father lived. They started after the first visit from Dunstan's men."

"By tomorrow, you'll be free of that man. There will be no cause for the dreams to come after that."

She shuddered. "Aye," she answered slowly. "It's just that..."

He brushed her forehead with his lips and whispered, "Just that what?"

"You'll think me foolish."

"Nay, tell me."

The warmth of his arms cuddling her made her feel so safe that she felt foolish at voicing the thought. "It's old Maeve. She did say that I would be forced to marry against my will."

"She also said that the moon would turn to blood, or some such nonsense, as I recollect. Sweetheart, you can't let the ravings of an old woman upset you."

"'Tis only that Maeve's ravings, as you call them, usually turn out to be true."

Thomas smiled. "This time they won't. Tomorrow we deliver the tax to Dunstan Castle and that's the last you ever have to even think about Baron Dunstan."

Alyce began to be aware that she was sitting on Thomas's thighs, her legs stretched out alongside his. There was pressure from his forearm against one of her breasts. The position was highly improper, but she made no move to shift away from him. In fact, she compounded the impropriety by letting her head drop onto his shoulder. "I hope so. I've heard enough monstrous tales of Philip of Dunstan to last me a lifetime."

For a moment neither said anything. Alyce closed her eyes and let herself enjoy the warmth their bodies generated against the frigid night air. She was wrapped in a blanket, as well as his arms, but Thomas had no covering. "Here," she said, tugging the blanket from around her. "You should have some of this, too. It's grown dreadfully cold."

Thomas laughed, but loosened his hold enough

to allow her to drape the blanket around both their shoulders. "I hadn't noticed," he said dryly. "At least not in these past few minutes."

"Aye, it's much warmer with two, isn't it?"

"Aye." His voice was mild, but behind the simple word she sensed a careful restraint. He made no move to do anything more than hold her.

"Are we near dawn?" she asked. "I don't think I've ever been outside at such an hour."

He looked up at the sky. The inky blackness had faded, but it was still possible to see a smattering of stars. "There's time yet. Do you think you could fall back to sleep?"

"Nay. This is much nicer, sitting here with you. Unless your arms are tired?"

"My arms are not the problem, sweetheart."

Misunderstanding him, she wriggled, trying to relieve him of her weight. The effort only elicited a groan from him.

"I should get up," she said at once. "I'm too heavy to be cradled like a babe."

"You're not heavy," Thomas murmured. "But it's very clear that I hold in my arms a woman grown, not a babe."

This time she caught the unmistakable note in his voice. She pulled back a little to gaze directly into his eyes. Her lips parted slightly, of their own accord. She held in a breath.

Then he turned her slightly in his arms, lowered his head and kissed her.

Chapter Seven

Thomas had been fighting his desire all day long as she rode beside him, straight and proud in the saddle, and then throughout the night as he watched her relaxed in sleep. It was foolhardy and wrong, but, by the rood, he could no longer help himself. He promised it would be no more than a kiss, but the instant their lips touched, all rational thought fled.

She appeared to have no objection to his caresses. She wound her arms around him and allowed their bodies to come together in an intimate intertwining, as if seeking the greatest possible contact. His mouth stayed joined with hers as they ended up lying on the ground, Alyce underneath and Thomas on top, touching from feet to chest. He continued to drink kisses from her mouth, one after another, deep and then light, until he felt quite drunk from them.

It seemed to be having much the same effect on Alyce. She laughed low in her throat, and her words were slurred as she murmured, ''I believe you're the one who acquired a potion from Maeve, for surely I'm drugged.''

He pulled back and allowed some of the cold night air to cool their heated bodies. ''I feel it, too, sweetheart. But 'tis the lovemaking that drugs us, not any herb.''

She let out a deep breath. ''I'm learning why people are fools for love. 'Tis wondrous.''

''Aye. It's easy to forget all else when under Eros's spell.'' Thomas rolled to one side of her, keeping her head cradled on one arm. ''But don't worry, I've sworn a knightly oath not to take advantage of any of the damsels in distress that I choose to aid.''

Alyce lifted her head. ''You have?''

To Thomas's surprise, she sounded almost angry. Confused, he answered, ''Er…aye, I have.''

Pushing on his chest for balance, she sat up. ''Let me see if I understand you. You have nobly come to the rescue of a damsel in distress, that damsel being me.'' She cocked her head to one side, considering. ''Aye, I suppose I have to agree that you've come to my rescue, more or less.''

He sat up beside her. ''You sound as if you're not happy with the idea.''

''Oh, I'm happy enough, and grateful to you. I

just hadn't realized there were conditions attached to being one of your needy damsels.''

Now Thomas was thoroughly confused. He could see how she would be angry if he had requested sexual favors as a condition to his aid, but, given his chivalrous declaration that he would *not* take advantage of her, he could see absolutely no reason for her ire. ''There are no conditions,'' he said.

''Except that you don't want to make love to me.''

Thomas threw up his hands in exasperation. For the dozenth time, he realized that Alyce of Sherborne was like no female he'd ever encountered. ''My sweet Alyce, if you were a little more experienced in these matters, you would have noticed compelling evidence that I very *much* want to make love to you. But I can't.''

This made her pause a moment before she replied carefully, ''Oh, I'm sorry. Is it…some kind of war wound?''

Thomas gave a hearty laugh. ''It's no wound that keeps me celibate this night with a delectable lady within arm's reach. 'Tis that the lady in question is a noblewoman, ward to the king.'' He reached out and took a gentle grasp on her chin. ''I believe you're too innocent to realize what trouble you could cause yourself with this kind of a game. For a woman of your station, your virginity must be for your husband and none other.''

She gave an irritated huff. "It's not for you nor the king nor any man to tell me what I can or can't do with my virginity."

"Alyce—" he protested, trying to interrupt, but she continued.

"What we had together here a few minutes ago was beautiful. And that day in the meadow, when you thought I was merely Rose, the serving girl. It felt so right for us to come together—"

"Aye, it did, but—"

"Then you turn all cold and businesslike and tell me that my body is meant for the man chosen for me by the king. You're no different than the men sent by Baron Dunstan, discussing my wedding and bedding as if I were a prize sow."

"I didn't mean—"

She jumped to her feet. "Well, fie on you, my chivalrous knight. I'll accept your aid, since it seems I have no choice in the matter, but I'll thank you to keep your hands and your advice to yourself from now on."

"Alyce, sweetheart, my intention was not—"

"And if I do end up having to marry Philip of Dunstan, I hope it'll set you tossing on your pallet at night to know that he is the one collecting this *prize* that I would have given to you freely."

"You can't know—" Thomas began. But before he could get out more than a few words, Alyce had marched away in the direction of the road.

He sat there a moment longer on the ground,

stunned. He'd had his face slapped before by a female for taking too many liberties. This was the first time he'd been dressed down for not taking *enough*.

Slowly he got to his feet. His still-racing body added its reproof to the one Alyce had given him. He'd had her warm and pliant and willing in his arms. She was right. What had possessed him to turn so chivalrous? Scowling, he made his way to the road.

He'd tried to do the noble thing, but all he'd accomplished was to make her angry. Now it was too late to do anything about it. When they reached Dunstan Castle, she'd be riding out of his life.

For the moment, he'd better go after her to be sure she didn't take a wrong turn and lose her way in the forest. As long as she was in his charge, he *was* going to take care of her, whether she wanted to be taken care of or not. But one thing was certain. If he ever had the lady of Sherborne in his arms again, he would follow the dictates of his body and his heart and let chivalry be damned.

They met Kenton and the others at a small church near Dunstan Castle. The priest who greeted them seemed to know Thomas, and ushered him immediately back to the sacristy, where Kenton was waiting.

As they entered, Kenton exclaimed, ''Two successful calls, Thomas. We've collected nearly enough—'' He broke off as he saw Alyce. ''What's she doing here? Are you daft, man?''

Thomas brushed off his friend's criticism. ''She's just come along to see the money safely here. Her men will be taking her back to Sherborne directly.''

Kenton remembered his manners enough to give Alyce a small bow, but he was obviously upset. ''Good day, Lady Alyce. I mean no offense, but this is no task for a female. I don't like seeing you here, a stone's throw from Dunstan Castle.''

''Nor do I,'' Thomas agreed curtly. Turning to her, he added, ''You and your men have seen me and the money safely here. Now you can be on your way back.''

All morning Alyce had been regretting her harsh words of the previous evening, but she hadn't known how to make up for them. Impulsiveness had always been one of her faults. In the cold light of day, she could see that Thomas had indeed been trying to protect her welfare. She was virtually certain that he had wanted to continue their lovemaking just as she had, but he had restrained himself for her sake. She should have thanked him instead of berating him.

But he'd been aloof and distant, speaking only when necessary to get them to their destination. So she'd remained silent as well, and the gulf between them had widened.

Now he wanted her to leave without so much as

a moment in private to settle their quarrel. She found the idea intolerable.

"I'll stay until the money is safely delivered," she said.

"Fant—" Kenton began to say a name, then stopped and substituted, "The man who will take the money to Dunstan is not here yet. We may have hours to wait yet. It would be best for you to be on your way back, milady."

Alyce looked at Thomas, who nodded his head in agreement. "You promised that you would do as I asked," he reminded her.

"Aye, and you promised that I could see the money to its destination."

"Which is here, lass. We've reached Dunstan."

She gave a stubborn shake of her head. "We're *near* Dunstan, but the money has not yet reached the castle gates."

Kenton's irritation over her presence was evidently overcome by his amusement at watching his friend spar with her. "I've warned you about bargaining with crafty negotiators, Thomas," he said with a grin.

Thomas looked as if he'd like to throttle both Alyce and his lieutenant, but his voice remained calm as he said to her, "We'll rest here until our man arrives to take in the money. You and your men may stay, but as soon as the messenger gets here, you're to head back. At that point we won't be able to worry about you anymore. We'll have to concentrate on getting the ransom money back from Dunstan.''

Alyce looked out the tall sacristy window toward the imposing castle on the horizon. "Is he there at the castle now?" she asked.

Thomas looked at the priest, who nodded and said, "Aye, the baron is currently in residence, milady."

A chill went through her. She was less than a league away from the shadow that had loomed over her life this past year. If Thomas was right, after today she would be free of him. It was hard to believe.

"All the more reason for you to leave quickly, Lady Alyce," Thomas said.

He sounded like a soldier giving orders. There was not the least reminder of the mellow-voiced charmer who had whispered in her ear last night and drugged her with his kisses. Obviously, he was done with his dalliance, finished with the pleasant distraction he had found along the road, and ready to get back to his work. So be it, she thought.

She answered stiffly, "My men and I will rest here for a few hours, then we'll start back. I won't 'bother' you further."

Thomas nodded, not appearing to notice the coldness of her tone, then he put his hand on Kenton's shoulder, and the two men started toward the door. "Tell me about the collections," he said.

They exited the room, immersed in discussion,

leaving Alyce standing alone in the middle of the empty sacristy. Obviously, Thomas thought this was over—this brief journey they'd allowed themselves into the world of infatuation. Like a worthy soldier, he would walk away unscarred. But she wasn't sure that she was ready to give up the battle. He'd turned cold and distant, but she at least wanted the chance to try to talk with him about what had happened between them.

She lifted her head, straightened her shoulders and left to find her men.

They'd waited all day, but the messenger they looked for had not come. When Alyce had tried to question Thomas about the man, he'd told her, reluctantly, that it was a supporter of King Richard working inside Dunstan Castle.

"It's safer for both him and you if you don't even know his name, Alyce. But rest assured he will see that the money is delivered, and bring written proof of it so that Dunstan and Prince John cannot try to claim that they never received it."

"I'd like to meet the man and offer him my thanks for his help," Alyce said.

"It would not be wise, milady," Thomas answered briefly. "I'll let him know of your gratitude."

Alyce, Thomas, his men and the Sherborne guards were all waiting in the single-room living quarters that adjoined the church. Thomas had kept busy all afternoon, and Alyce had still not had a moment alone with him. In their few exchanges, his voice had been so formal and distant that she had not seen an opportunity to bring up a topic as intimate as what had transpired between the two of them. But the messenger could arrive any moment. If she was going to make amends, it would have to be quick.

"Might we speak together in private?" she asked in a low voice.

Thomas looked around the cramped quarters. "I should be making plans with Kenton. Is there something in particular you needed?"

She lowered her voice further. "It's about last night—"

"I tried at the time to offer my apologies, though, in truth, I wasn't entirely sure what I was apologizing for. I believe it was for trying to protect your virtue."

The three Sherborne guards were playing a dice game on the floor, practically at their feet. Alyce edged toward the door of the room. "Could we not step outside a moment?"

Thomas shrugged and stooped under the low lintel to follow her out into the afternoon sunlight. When they were alone, he said, "I had no intention of offending you, Alyce. That's the last thing I wanted."

She was relieved to hear the return of a touch of warmth to his voice. "That's why I needed to

talk with you. I—I was wrong to be angry. You
see, I haven't had much experience in these matters
and I…'' She stopped. How did a well-bred lady
tell a man that she had desired him, that her body
had been betraying her with an urgency she hardly
understood?

He gave a tired smile. ''And in the cold light of
day you've realized that I was very right to call a
halt to things when I did.''

That was not what she wanted to say at all, but
before she could try to reformulate her words, Kenton came striding toward them from around the
church.

''He's sent word, Thomas. They've been watching him too carefully. He feels that he's under suspicion, and it would be too risky for him to come
out to us right now.''

Thomas's expression turned grim. ''Your messenger?'' Alyce asked.

Kenton nodded and asked, ''So what do we do
now?''

''We can't afford more delay,'' Thomas answered. ''I'll take the money in myself.''

Kenton stared. ''Now I know you've gone daft.
Dunstan'll spot you in an instant.''

''You've met him?'' Alyce asked, surprised.

The men ignored her question. ''I'll pretend I'm
just a worker from Sherborne and present the gold
to the castle warden. I won't have to see Dunstan
himself.''

"But he could see you, Thomas. If you run into him, he'll know you in an instant. Let me go."

Thomas shook his head. "Dunstan could recognize you as well, Kenton. No, I'll be the one to risk it."

Kenton gave a huff of exasperation. "That's insane. Any of the men could go. He'd be less likely to know them."

"How have you known Dunstan?" Alyce asked more insistently.

Thomas continued to ignore her. "There's no discussion, Kenton. I'll be the one to go."

Alyce cleared her throat and spoke loudly. "Would someone listen to me? If Dunstan knows all of you, then I'll deliver the money to him. 'Tis what I wanted to do in the first place, to confront the monster myself. I deserve to see the expression on his face, after all the trouble he's put me to in the past year."

Thomas and Kenton scarcely glanced at her, obviously thinking her offer too ridiculous for comment.

Thomas turned to go back inside. "We'll discuss this with the others and work out a plan in case things don't go well. Shall I go tonight, do you think?"

Kenton followed his leader inside. "The men will be as against your going as I am. But it's almost dark. We can't do anything now until morning. Perhaps by then Fantierre will be able to do the job himself.''

They disappeared inside and someone closed the door behind them. Once again, Alyce was left standing by herself.

"Now, you all understand that you don't have to do this thing? I'll not hold it against you if you prefer not to go ahead with it.'' Alyce leaned toward the three men who were watching her with adoring gazes.

Fredrick answered for the three of them. ''We'll do whatever ye say, milady. That's why we've come.''

Hugh and Guelph nodded in agreement.

Alyce felt her heart speed up with excitement. "Then here's the plan. I've told Sir Thomas that we're leaving for home. In fact, we are heading home. We'll just make a stop on the way—at Dunstan Castle.''

"How will we get the money, milady?'' Hugh asked.

"We'll simply take it. The chests are sitting unguarded in the sacristy. We need only one of them. It appears to be Sir Thomas's custom to leave quantities of money around unattended.''

Fredrick frowned. ''Beggin' yer ladyship's pardon, but we'd feel a mite better if ye'd let the three of us go by ourselves. Who knows what they'll say at the castle when a noble lady comes riding in?''

"Precisely." Alyce's eyes danced. "Which is why there will only be three lads from Sherborne delivering the money. You, Fredrick. And you, Hugh. And...*me!*"

"The three of us will go?" Fredrick asked. "Milady, I wish ye wouldn't—"

"Aye." She interrupted him and turned to Guelph. "You'll keep watch at the gates, Guelph, while we three go inside."

Guelph nodded without speaking. The slightest of the young men and painfully shy, he spoke so rarely that Alyce wasn't sure she would recognize his voice.

"Three *lads,* ye said, milady." Fredrick's tone was wary.

"Aye, three lads." She turned again to Guelph. "I have one more favor to ask of you, Guelph," she told him. When he gave another silent nod, she continued, "I'll need to borrow your clothes."

She knew deep down that this, her greatest adventure yet, was also the most foolhardy. But what could be the harm? No one would recognize the slender boy in the dirty tunic and old felt hat as the lady of Sherborne.

They would deliver the money to the castle warden, demand a receipt in exchange and be on their way. As Thomas had said, they most likely would never even set eyes on the baron. But secretly, she hoped to catch at least a glimpse of him.

When they were finished, they'd stop back at the church to notify Sir Thomas and his men that the mission had been accomplished. Thomas would be livid. She could hardly wait to see his face, she thought with a mischievous grin.

They'd had to hurry. By the time they'd collected the chest of gold and made the exchange of clothes, leaving poor Guelph draped in little more than a blanket, it was well after sunset. The castle gates had already been closed, but there were still guards manning them. When the trio said they came from Sherborne and asked to see the castle warden, the guard admitted them.

The castle was guarded by a portcullis with a wicked spiked bottom. Alyce looked up at it as they rode underneath. Sudden fear hollowed out her stomach as she realized for the first time the danger she and her men might be riding into.

Once inside the gates, two castle guards in Dunstan livery came for their horses, and a third ushered them into a small shed outside the castle keep. It appeared to be more of a tack room than any kind of accounting chamber.

"Be sure they know 'tis the warden we need to see," Alyce told Fredrick in an urgent whisper.

"Aye, milady."

"Shh," she cautioned him. "My name's Guelph, remember?"

Fredrick's gaunt face reflected her own sudden unease with the whole plan, but he staunchly addressed the guard and demanded once again to have an audience with the baron's money man or the castle bailiff. Then he set the leather chest he carried down on the dirt floor.

Then they waited, shifting nervously on their feet. The room was dim, lit by one small torch. Alyce's discomfort grew as the time stretched out. If the guards hadn't disappeared with their mounts, she'd be tempted to jump back on her horse and flee.

"The bailiff be taking a long time to come," Hugh said finally.

"I suspect he's a busy man," Alyce said, trying to reassure herself as much as the two men. "This is a much more important castle than Sherborne."

"They saw we had no weapons," Fredrick observed. "I can't see how they would be suspicious."

Still no one came. Alyce's feet began to feel pinched in Guelph's stiff boots. She looked around the room, wondering if she should sit on one of the barrels that lined the wall. She had taken one step toward them when there was a flare of light behind her. Turning, she saw that two guards had entered the room, each carrying a blazing torch. Just behind them came a gray-haired man in a long, wine-colored tunic. "What is this story of gold from Sherborne?" the man asked imperiously.

Fredrick's voice cracked. "'Tis the tax, yer worship. For milady. The lady Alyce. 'Tis the tax for Prince John so she won't have to marry the baron.'' His words grew stronger the longer he spoke. By the time he finished, he sounded almost as imperious as the red-cloaked man. ''And we'd ask yer worship to give us a paper with yer seal to show that it was safely delivered here.''

The man took a couple steps toward Fredrick. ''Who are you?'' he asked.

''I'm Fredrick,'' he answered. He looked awkward as he gave an uncertain bow, but spoke firmly to add, ''Fredrick of Sherborne Castle.''

The man glanced at the other two visitors, but, to Alyce's relief, seemed to take little notice of them. ''Who sent you?'' he asked Fredrick, his voice echoing off the stone walls.

Fredrick didn't flinch. ''We come from the lady Alyce. To deliver her tax.''

The man in red looked down at the chest. He motioned to a Dunstan guard who was standing just behind him. ''Open it,'' he said.

The man scrambled to obey, but was evidently not quick enough for his master, since as soon as the chest lay open, the tall man lifted a booted foot and kicked the soldier to one side, sending him sprawling in the dust.

There was a moment of silence as every eye in the room was trained on the mound of gold coins.

''Where did the money come from?'' the man in red asked Fredrick.

He had no answer for this. Alyce sent up a silent prayer that he would have enough sense not to mention the Havilland knights.

''I don't know, yer worship…er…yer lordship.'' The man had not introduced himself, so Fredrick was unsure of how to address him. ''My orders was just to bring the gold and get proof of delivery for the lady Alyce.''

Alyce was studying the tall man. He was wearing a heavy gold chain around his neck and a ring the size of an almond on his finger. This was no accountant or warden, she realized. This man was rich and likely noble. Some would call his features handsome, but the lines in his face were deeply etched, as though carved into a perpetual scowl.

The lines twisted as he said with a cruel smile, ''Well, Fredrick of Sherborne, mayhap if your friends here see your tongue ripped from your mouth, their memory will prove better than yours.''

Fredrick swayed backward, his skin growing pale. The face of the man towering over him seemed to glow as he watched his victim cower.

All at once Alyce knew without a doubt that the monster who was standing just a few feet away from her, tormenting her guard, was none other than Baron Dunstan himself.

The fear in her stomach weighed like a ball of lead, but she wasn't about to let her men be hurt because of her reckless behavior. She would have to step forward and reveal herself to Dunstan. The thought terrified her. Now that she had seen his face, she realized that it would be frightening to be the recipient of Baron Dunstan's anger. But she was a noblewoman in liege to King Richard. She didn't think even Dunstan would dare hurt her.

She opened her mouth to speak, but before she could get the words out, the baron gave an exclamation of disgust. "It's too late at night to waste my time on fools," he said. Speaking to the guards, he growled, "Throw them in the dungeon." Then he whirled around, his scarlet robes billowing around him, and stalked from the room.

Chapter Eight

Thomas stood with his hands on his hips and stared at the shaken young man in front of him, dressed only in hose and a blanket. "What do they call you, lad?"

"Guelph, sir."

"Tell me again, slowly, Guelph. You say the lady Alyce went into Dunstan Castle? You saw her go inside?"

The guard nodded, clutching the blanket around him. He stood just outside the doorway of the priest's residence, where he'd timidly knocked moments before.

Thomas spoke through clenched teeth. "By the saints, I swear I'm going to wring her lovely neck, if Dunstan hasn't already done me the service."

"They wasn't planning to see the baron or anything, sir. They was just planning to leave the money. 'Twould be safer for us to do it, milady said, to not risk the baron recognizing any of ye."

"How long have they been in there?" he asked, struggling to keep the panic he felt out of his voice.

"I reckon 'twas near sundown, sir. We thought we'd be on the road back to Sherborne long before now. When they didn't come out after so long, I thought I'd better come to ye."

"The first sensible thing you've done," Thomas snapped, some of his anger escaping. "How could you let her go in there—you and your friends?"

Guelph stared at the ground. "I'm truly sorry, yer lordship, but at Sherborne when Lady Alyce says something, well, then, that's what we do. There's not a man of us wouldn't give our life for her."

Thomas let out a long stream of air. "Let's just hope that no lives have to be given this night, Guelph."

"The baron Dunstan wouldn't hurt her ladyship once he knows who she is, would he?"

"Philip of Dunstan would put his own mother to the stake if the mood struck him." The guard, who couldn't have been much more than fifteen years old, looked as if he was about to cry. "Go see if you can find yourself some clothes, Guelph, while I decide what we're to do about this," Thomas added.

"If ye're planning to go to the castle, I want to go with ye," the guard said. "I'm good with the bow."

Thomas nodded absently, his mind whirring

with plans. "You can't go anywhere half-naked, boy. Get yourself dressed."

Guelph nodded vigorously, then trotted off in the direction of the church.

Dunstan's guards had put them in a dank, dark room that smelled of stale body odors and human terror. All the way across the bailey and down the tiny stairway to the place, Alyce had debated whether she should reveal herself. Surely even Philip of Dunstan would not dare throw a noble-woman into a place like this.

But then she'd remember his face as he'd kicked his own guard, the gleam in his eye when he had talked of ripping out Fredrick's tongue. Who knew what such a monster would do? Perhaps it would go worse for them all if he discovered that she had come herself, in disguise, with the gold that would relieve her from marrying him.

"Don't tell him, milady," Fredrick had urged. "The man's evil. I could see it in his eyes."

"I think you're right, Fredrick," she agreed. "But we've got to do something. By tomorrow he might have decided to kill us or to leave us here until our bones rot."

She quickly decided that it was probably fortu-nate that the hole they were in was dark. It was easier to stay here without being able to see what else shared their cell. It was entirely possible that they actually would find bones of other unfortunate souls who had been thrown into this place, never to be seen again. But the blackness was, fortunately, complete. The only proof that their accommodations were not empty was the scratching of tiny creatures scurrying around the stone walls.

Hugh observed calmly, "Rottin' wouldn't take long in a place like this."

"Oh, my friends," Alyce exclaimed. "It's my fault you are here. I thought I was helping, but it was foolhardy of me to try it. Now Thomas won't even know what's happened to us."

"Aye, he'll know," Hugh said. "I reckon Guelph will already have told him."

Alyce closed her eyes, though the blackness was the same, closed or open. Thomas would be furious with her, and with just cause. She'd risked her own life and the lives of her men to satisfy her own curiosity.

"I swear by St. Anne that when we get out of this mess, I'm going to go home to Sherborne and spend all day with Lettie making tapestries," she said.

She couldn't see Fredrick's face, but she could hear the smile in his voice as he replied, "Now that would be a sight to see, milady."

None of the three had sat down. The floor was dirt and felt slightly mushy. Alyce sighed. They wouldn't be able to keep standing the entire night.

"Are we in the middle of the room, do you think?" she asked.

She could hear the sound of Hugh walking, then running his hands over the stone. "There's a wall here, milady. And here. Aye, I reckon ye're in the middle." His foot hit some debris in the dark. "And I'd advise ye to stay right there," he added.

Slowly she sank to the ground, feeling with her hands to be sure she was not sitting on anything more undesirable than mud. "Maybe if you two sit down beside me and we lean up against each other," she said, "we can manage to get a little sleep."

"Hugh and me, leaning right up against ye, milady?" Fredrick sounded shocked. "Why, it wouldn't be decent."

"I'm afraid I never learned the proper etiquette for dungeons, Fredrick. So let's just let practicality rule the day. Come on now, we'll sit back to back."

In a moment she could feel the two men seating themselves behind her. She reached back and felt two strong shoulders. "This will work," she said. "Lean back and try not to think too much. Let's see who will be the first to fall asleep."

Her words were meant to be comforting. She had no illusions that she would be able to fall asleep under such conditions. But out on the road the night before, she'd slept poorly, and the events of the past two days had left her exhausted. As she felt the regular breathing of Hugh and Fredrick against her back, she closed her eyes and drifted to sleep.

It was taking entirely too long, Thomas thought again, swallowing down the bitter taste of fear in his throat. By the time the priest had fetched their inside man from the castle, it was nearly midnight. Thomas was pacing the floor of the priest's cramped quarters. Kenton had had to restrain him more than once from charging over to Dunstan Castle and demanding entrance all by himself.

"If Dunstan has discovered her disguise, God knows what he's doing to her," he'd told his lieutenant, tormented by the thought.

"Your Alyce is a clever girl, Thomas. We'll hope she knew enough not to let them see who she was."

"She's not *my* Alyce," Thomas grumbled. But he continued to pace and slap his hand nervously against his thigh, as though wishing he were at that moment drawing a sword to skewer Philip of Dunstan.

The supporter of Richard who had been working at Dunstan Castle was a tall, thin knight named Fantierre. Originally from Paris, he had become an early follower of the idealistic young king. When Richard had decided to embark on his Crusade, leaving the country to the mercy of his brother, Fantierre had accepted the dangerous assignment of staying on in England as one of Richard's undercover men, watching out for the interests of the true king.

"Your lady is very foolish," Fantierre told Thomas when he finally arrived at the church. "Dunstan could easily have killed the three of them without asking further questions."

"She's not *my* lady," Thomas corrected. "But, aye, if they come to no more harm than a few hours in the dungeon, they are lucky. In fact," he added grimly, "it just might do her some good."

Fantierre ignored Thomas's disclaimer. With a Gallic twinkle in his black eyes, he said, "Ah, young love. It can be pure torment, can it not?"

Thomas didn't have time to argue the point. If Fantierre was right, it appeared that Alyce had as yet come to no harm, but as soon as it was daybreak, there would again be the chance that her masquerade would be discovered. Then she would be at Dunstan's mercy.

In the darkest hours of early morning, Fantierre led them to a spot where they could scale the castle wall.

"No one expects trouble at Dunstan," Fantierre told them. "The garrison is small and, except for two guards at the gate, generally sleeps through the night."

Seasoned soldiers, Thomas's men moved without a sound over the wall and through the quiet castle grounds.

"This is too easy," Kenton said exultantly.

The crude plan they'd devised had assigned Kenton and Harry the Stout to find the money chest. According to Fantierre, the gold hadn't yet been moved into the castle. Kenton signaled silently to Thomas that he would be about his task. Thomas nodded agreement, then he and the other men followed Fantierre across the bailey and down the stairs to the dungeon.

Once again, there appeared to be no guards anywhere.

"Kenton was right," Thomas whispered. "It's almost too easy."

Fantierre cautioned, "The door will be locked. We might not be able to avoid making a noise in opening it, which could draw attention."

Thomas shrugged. "We have no choice. We've got to get them out—whatever it takes."

But here again they were lucky. The door was held closed with nothing more than a thick slab of wood. While that made it impossible to open from inside, from without the process was simple.

Fantierre slipped the bar out of the brace himself, then turned to Thomas. "Will you do the honors, Brand?" he asked. "Your fair lady awaits."

Thomas gave the Frenchman a quick smile, then stepped up to push open the thick door. Behind him, one of his men carried a small torch, which barely illuminated the horrible little room they'd just opened.

The stench was the first thing that hit Thomas.

Lord, to think of Alyce in such a place. Then he saw her, huddled on the floor with the two Sherborne men, looking pitiful and small. His heart cracked. All the angry words that he'd been rehearsing fled. He ran to her and lifted her in his arms, holding her tightly against his chest.

Her arms went around him and he felt her breast heave with a silent sob as she gasped, "Thomas."

"Are you all right? You're not hurt?"

"Nay, but I'm so sorry, Thomas. I never thought—"

"Hush," he said, cradling her another moment before he set her on her feet. "Not now. We'll talk later, but first we all need to get out of here."

He turned her toward the door, where Fantierre was watching them with a roguish smile. "The lovers united," he said.

Thomas shook his head in exasperation. "Alyce, this romantic gentleman is Fantierre. He led us in here to you."

Alyce gave the French knight a grateful smile and he responded with an elegant half bow. But there was no time for social niceties. Moving quickly and silently, they made their way back up the narrow stairs to the bailey.

Kenton and Harry stood at the top of the stairs, great grins on their faces. Harry held the treasure chest.

"Good work!" Thomas said softly as the entire group made its way back across the castle yard.

"Slick as peeling a plum," Kenton said. He boosted himself up on the wall and then turned to help Alyce. As Thomas lifted her up by her feet, Kenton pulled her up beside him. "Old Dunstan will be spitting fire when he discovers his prisoners are gone and the money as well."

"Quiet," Thomas ordered from down below, but the warning came too late. Out of the gloom of the night a guard appeared behind them on the wall. Kenton whirled around to face the man.

In an instant, Thomas had jumped up beside his lieutenant, and before the guard had time to cry out, he drew back his arm and smashed him in the face with the heavy iron hilt of his hunting knife.

Alyce watched in horror as the man sank to the ground, blood gushing from the socket of his eye. For a moment, she stood frozen.

"Come on," Thomas said. "Others may have heard."

Her gaze was still on the fallen man. His entire left check was caved inward. She felt as if she were going to be sick. Then Thomas seized her by the shoulders and she was being half pushed, half carried over the wall.

"Hurry," he urged when they reached the ground. With him holding one of her arms and Kenton the other, they ran across the dry moat and through a grove of trees. Thomas's men had retrieved the Sherborne horses and all the mounts were waiting on the other side. Silently, they mounted and rode back to the church.

The final encounter with the guard had dimmed some of their enthusiasm, but Kenton still sounded triumphant as they dismounted and took stock to be sure that everyone was accounted for. "Mission accomplished, men. Well done," he said.

Fantierre's expression was less victorious. "I just hope Dunstan doesn't try to seek revenge on Sherborne for this night's work."

Thomas nodded soberly in agreement.

"He might say that I'm obligated to marry him after all," Alyce suggested. "Since he didn't end up with the money."

Thomas shook his head. "At the very least, it will delay the matter. You just sit tight at Sherborne and send word to Prince John that you have three witnesses to testify that the money was delivered safely into Dunstan's hands. If they've lost track of it since then, it's their fault, not yours."

Fantierre looked remorseful. "It would have been better if I'd been able to get away this afternoon to take charge of things, as we'd planned."

"There's no point in recriminations," Thomas said. "The deed's done. And all we really needed was to buy Lady Alyce a little time. Soon King Richard will be back and none of John's scheming will make any difference."

A glow of light was showing on the eastern horizon. Fantierre looked toward it, his thin face thoughtful. "We will buy your lady that time, my friend. And, as you say, when Richard returns, it will be a better England for all of us. Now I must go back."

"Oh, surely you'll not go back to the castle," Alyce exclaimed. "What if they know you were the one who led Thomas in tonight?"

Fantierre laughed and reached for her hand. Though she was grimy and still wearing men's clothes, he lifted her fingers to his mouth and planted a kiss on them as if the two of them were in the most elegant salon in Paris. "Don't fret about me, *ma chère*. I've managed to ward off Dunstan's suspicions thus far. Any day now, Richard will return and I can throw off the mask I'm forced to wear, pretending to be loyal to that cur Dunstan and his master, John."

He turned to offer a hand to Thomas, who grasped it with both of his. Then with another one of his unmistakably foreign bows, he whirled around and strode off into the brightening dawn.

"I'm afraid for him, Thomas," Alyce said after he was gone.

"Aye, he barters the devil for his life each day, but, as he said, it shouldn't be so for too much longer."

Kenton came up beside them. "We're ready to ride, Thomas. The coin is safely loaded. It's all there."

Thomas nodded. "I'm changing plans slightly, Kenton. I'll meet you and the men in Dover."

Kenton looked surprised. His glance slid to Alyce. "Thomas, we don't have time—" he began.

Thomas interrupted him. "I'll not tarry. I'll ride with the lady Alyce back to Sherborne, but I promise, you'll see me in Dover shortly after you arrive yourself."

Alyce tried to protest. "My men will see me safely back…"

Neither man paid her any attention. "You know the meeting place?" Thomas asked.

Kenton's expression was disapproving, but he made no further argument. "Aye. How long should we wait for you?"

Thomas took Alyce's arm, turned her abruptly around and began pulling her toward the horses. Over his shoulder, he answered curtly, "You won't have to wait for me."

"I know you're angry with me," Alyce said to Thomas finally, after they'd traveled for half the morning without speaking. The two of them were riding a few yards ahead of the three Sherborne guards.

Thomas glanced over at her. "'Twas a damn fool escapade, but I blame myself for letting you come with me in the first place."

"I insisted on coming."

"Aye, you did."

They rode in silence for another few moments, then Alyce said, "I'm sorry."

"We're fortunate that no ill came of the episode."

"But it did. That poor guard's face." She shuddered. "And I wish your friend Fantierre had not had to go back there."

"He knows what he's doing."

Alyce sighed. Obviously, nothing she could say was going to soften Thomas's anger, which even she admitted was well deserved. She made one more attempt. "At least you got all the money back safely for Richard."

"Aye." This time he did not even look at her.

"I intend to send word to Prince John, telling him that I paid my tax, that my messengers were treated abominably in the bargain, and that I don't expect to be bothered by him again."

This elicited a small smile from Thomas. "No doubt the prince will be less than pleased with that message."

"I don't care. As you yourself have said, he's not the king. He never should have arranged a marriage for me in the first place."

"You already have one powerful man angry with you. It might not be wise to raise Prince John's ire as well. If he gets angry enough, he could decide to give Dunstan what he wants—tax or no tax."

Alyce sighed. "Then I'm no better off than I was before. I'm still at the mercy of unscrupulous men who will do what they want with me."

Thomas pulled his horse to a halt just as the road neared a small stream. Fredrick, Hugh and Guelph rode up beside them. "We'll stop here for rest and water," Thomas said.

The three guards dismounted and led their horses down the grassy bank. Thomas jumped off his stallion and walked over to Alyce, holding his arms up to her.

"I'm beginning to think 'twould be divine justice to let Dunstan have you," he said, "but unfortunately, I wouldn't be able to stomach the thought of it. So I guess I'll have to make sure it doesn't happen."

Alyce gave an indignant huff. Thomas had come to her aid, but his attitude told her that he was just one more male trying to control the way she wanted to live her life.

"And just how do you intend to do that, Sir Thomas of Havilland? I thought you were leaving directly to meet your men in Dover."

"I am."

"And from there you will be taking Richard's ransom to the Continent."

"That's right."

"Which makes you a rather unlikely protector to keep me from any schemes that Dunstan and Prince John might devise."

Thomas was still holding his arms up to help her down, but she refused to move. "Get down," he ordered. "If you don't need the rest, your horse does."

Reluctantly, she let him help her off. "You have no answer for that one, do you? How does a knight protect his lady when he's not even in the same country?"

She could see that her words disturbed him, but his answer was calm and deliberate. "He's considering locking her away in a tower somewhere," he said grimly. "But the first thing that he does is make sure that the lady understands that she does, indeed, belong to *him*."

Alyce opened her mouth to ask him what he meant by that remark, but he had already marched down the bank toward the stream.

Philip of Dunstan paced the length of his armory, the captain of his castle guard standing at attention in front of him. "Am I to be cursed with idiots at every turn?" Dunstan asked.

The captain remained silent, uncertain how to reply.

"Am I?" Dunstan roared.

"Ah, nay, milord. That is, ah—"

"First the blundering fools who can't even carry out a simple assignment to take over a backcountry castle." Dunstan threw out a long arm and sent a pile of weapons clattering to the floor. "They let themselves be outwitted by a slip of a girl.'' He stabbed his captain with a gaze. ''Do you have a single soldier who's worth the food we feed him?''

The captain swallowed painfully. ''Aye, milord. You have many good men in your ranks. I believe if you'd let me pick a contingent to go to Sherborne—''

Dunstan shook his head in disgust. ''Nay, I'm going to have to handle it myself. I should have done it long ago.''

''You'll go to Sherborne, milord?''

''Aye. 'Tis past time I paid a visit to my charming bride-to-be.''

''Very good, milord,'' the captain said. ''About tonight. Of course, I'll be disciplining the guards—''

Suddenly Dunstan held up his hand and stopped pacing. ''We have a traitor,'' he said slowly, his eyes narrowing. ''Someone led those men into the castle tonight.''

''Aye, milord. I'm afraid you might be right.''

''A filthy, bloody traitor,'' Dunstan repeated, running his hand over the sharp edge of a sword that was mounted in one of the wall racks.

''Do you think it's someone working for Richard?'' the captain asked.

Dunstan shot him an exasperated glance. ''Of course he's Richard's man. I want him found.''

The captain bowed. ''Aye, milord.''

''But don't kill him.''

''Milord?''

''Find him and bring him to me. I want the plea-sure of skewering the bastard myself.''

Lettie fussed around Alyce as if she had been brought back from the edge of Hades, which wasn't too far from the truth, Alyce thought, shud-dering as she remembered her night in the bowels of Dunstan Castle. She had sworn Fredrick, Hugh and Guelph to secrecy on the details of the adven-ture, but it was obvious to her old nurse that she had been through some kind of an ordeal.

The arduous ride had not been conducive to con-versation, so Alyce had been left to ponder the meaning of Thomas's remark beside the stream. He wanted to be sure she knew that she belonged to him, he'd said—words of a lover or a husband. But the remark had been made with a stern, almost angry demeanor, certainly not a loverlike expres-sion.

She had to admit that his words had caused a tingle to run along her limbs, much like the feeling she'd had when he'd first kissed her. But she didn't want to belong to him or to any man. Hadn't they just risked their lives on the botched tax delivery to prove just that?

They had not stopped on the way home. Thomas had kept pushing them through the entire night. By the time they'd arrived at Sherborne, after nearly two days with no sleep, they were exhausted and aching. Alyce had been barely civil to him as she'd offered him a bed to rest in before he started the trip to Dover.

"Thank you," he'd answered, equally short. "I do need to sleep, but I'll see you before I leave."

Without answering, she'd let Lettie lead her up to her chamber. Her nurse insisted that before her charge could seek her bed, she had to wash away the grime of the hard ride. Though Alyce was dizzy with fatigue, she found that it was satisfying to scrub her skin until it stung, knowing that she was washing away any remaining filth that still clung to her from the Dunstan jail.

Finally, the bathing was done. She donned a light night rail and, refusing the breakfast Lettie brought to her, fell onto her pallet. In spite of the bright morning sun streaming into the room, she was asleep within seconds.

The sun was reddish gold when she awoke in the late afternoon. A sound had awakened her. She opened her eyes to see Thomas standing just inside the door to her chamber.

Alyce sat up in bed, not alarmed exactly, but ill at ease. She had a feeling that she was finally about to receive the scolding she'd been expecting since her rescue at Dunstan. But Thomas's face did not look angry as he turned back to the door and closed the latch with a decisive click. It looked…determined.

"I'm sorry to have to wake you," he said, turning back to her and walking over to the bed, "but I have to leave soon for Dover, and we have some unfinished business to take care of before I go."

She looked up at him, surprised. "Business?"

"Aye." He took hold of her feet with one hand and moved them so that he could sit beside her on the bed. "As you pointed out back there on the road, you may still be in danger from Dunstan or Prince John or both. Do you remember our conversation?"

She remembered every word of it. "I still intend to send word to the prince, but I'll try to be diplomatic with my message. Is that what you're worried about?"

His gaze was roving over her. Suddenly she was aware that the thin lawn of her nightdress concealed little. She reached for the blanket to cover herself, but his hand stopped hers. "Leave it," he said, his voice low. "I like looking at you."

"'Tis not proper for you to be here—" she began.

"I don't intend for it to be proper," he said. "I don't intend for it to be proper at all."

Chapter Nine

Somewhere in her throat a pulse began to pound. She didn't need to ask what he meant by the words. The intensity of his eyes left no doubt that his thoughts were no longer on court intrigue or bride taxes.

"Thomas, you were the one who said this couldn't happen between us," she said, making her words as direct as his gaze.

"I've changed my mind."

His hand held hers prisoner against the blanket. She pulled away. "Perhaps I've changed mine as well," she said, but little tremors had begun deep in her middle.

"I don't think you have. You want this as much as I. We've both wanted it since the first moment we set eyes on one another. Do you deny it?"

Part of her wished he would stop talking and simply kiss her, as he had done before. The other part wanted to bolt from the bed and flee the room. Slowly, she shook her head. He held in a breath as he waited for her to say, "No, I don't deny it."

That was enough. He reached for her and lifted her to his lap. "I thought about this with every beat of my horse's hooves all the way from Dunstan to Sherborne," he said.

Alyce had had much the same feeling, but she didn't have time to tell him so before his lips closed over hers and he pushed her back on the bed. His wool tunic was rough and cold against the warm softness of her gown, but she hardly noticed, as all her feeling centered in the silky joining of their mouths.

Her breasts grew hard, and he responded by moving a hand to knead them softly through the thin gown. "I've long thought about doing this as well," he murmured. "I've spent long reveries thinking about it. Though in the best of them," he added with a smile, "they were bare."

As he spoke, he reached down to pull up the hem of her night rail. After a moment's hesitation, she moved to help him lift the dress over her head, leaving her naked.

He sat up and threw the dress aside, then looked down at her. "Even 'Rose' does not do justice to thy beauty, sweetheart," he said, his voice suddenly husky.

Strangely, she did not feel at all shy, lying there with his gaze on her. Even when he ran his hand slowly, almost reverently, from her knee to her breast, she felt no embarrassment. What had he said on the road that day? That he wanted to be sure she knew that she belonged to *him*. In that moment, she did know it. She belonged to Thomas Havilland, body and soul.

She closed her eyes and gave herself up to the feeling of his hands on her skin—delicious, sinful pleasures she had never felt before. Then he was naked, too, and it was not just his hands but his whole body that stroked hers, the scratchy hair of his thighs against her smoothness, the hard muscles of his chest against her pliant breasts.

"I don't want to hurt you, my love," he said. "We'll take as much time as you need."

But Alyce was feeling urges that did not allow for leisurely exploration. With a small whimper of longing, she tightened her arms around Thomas's back and settled her body firmly against his. Sensing her need, he readied her with practiced fingers, then entered her quickly, whispering words of encouragement in her ear.

She felt a slight sting, but it was soon gone, replaced by more urgent yearnings. "Shh, sweetheart, relax," he told her, moving with exquisite slowness. Just when Alyce thought she could not stand the wanting, it burst upon her, like dozens of shooting stars radiating from that special private spot where they were joined.

An exhalation of air and a tightening of his body

told her that Thomas, too, had found his release. Afterward, he dropped his head heavily to rest on her chest. She closed her eyes and lay quiet, loving the feel of the weight of his body all along the length of her.

It was several moments before he lifted his head. She gave him a tired, satisfied smile.

"My Rose is happy," he said, dropping a light kiss on the tip of her nose.

She nodded drowsily, but after a moment, she added, "I thought it would be more complicated than that."

He looked a little insulted. "I'm sorry to disappoint you."

"You misunderstand me. It was not at all disappointing. It was simple and right and...*wondrous.*"

He moved to one side and nestled her in his arms, her head on his shoulder. "Aye, it was that."

"I know nothing of lovemaking, but somehow I knew it would be like that between us. I was angry and hurt that night on the road. It seemed that, halfway to the goal, you decided that you were no longer interested."

Thomas chuckled. "I swear this must be the first time in history that a man has had recriminations for *not* taking advantage of a helpless female."

Alyce bristled. "I'm not a helpless female." When he smiled, she added, "I realize that I have managed to get myself into trouble a time or two

since you first met me, but you'll have to take my
word for it that I'm not usually helpless. After all,
I did ward off Dunstan's men for almost a year.''

''Sweetheart, I take back the words. You are,
indeed, one of the least helpless females I know.
But that still didn't make it right for me to seduce
you.''

Alyce refused to accept his characterization of
their lovemaking. ''I thought we were seducing
each other,'' she said firmly.

Thomas gave a snort of exasperation. ''That's
not the way it works,'' he said dryly.

''So what changed your mind? Why did you decide to make love to me tonight?''

He rose up on one elbow to look down at her
face. ''I told you on the road today.''

''You said that I belong to you.''

''Aye. You do. I've become convinced of it.
When I learned that you were imprisoned in Dunstan Castle, I knew that I couldn't have stood it if
Philip of Dunstan had taken what was destined to
be mine.''

As the flush of their lovemaking faded from her
cheeks, Alyce felt the first prickles of irritation.
''I'm a noblewoman in my own right, Thomas.
Mistress of Sherborne Castle. I've paid my tax to
the king so that I can be my own woman and belong to no man.''

''Aye, your obligation to the king is paid. So
now you need belong to no man but me.'' He gave

her one of his disarming grins, but somehow it was not enough to make the words palatable.

She sat up and said stiffly, "I need belong to no man—including you."

Still smiling, he put a proprietary hand on her stomach. "Shall I make love to you again to convince you?"

She pushed his hand away. "You sound like some kind of pillaging knight, gloating over a conquest. Is that what this is?"

Thomas's grin died as he sat up beside her. "Sweetheart, if this was a conquest, 'twas you who did the conquering. When I thought about you and Dunstan, I realized that you were meant to be with no one but me."

It was the second time he had mentioned Dunstan. She remembered now that Thomas had admitted he knew the baron. "How did you and Dunstan meet?" she asked.

"The baron rode with us on Crusade." His voice had stiffened.

"You were colleagues then?"

He grimaced. "We rode together."

"And you didn't get along."

He seemed reluctant to tell the story. "There was an incident," he said shortly.

"What kind of incident?" Somehow it seemed important for her to understand Thomas's past relationship with her would-be bridegroom.

"Some of our men were killed in an ambush by

Saladin's troops. Kenton and I think that Dunstan had sent word of our whereabouts to the enemy camp.''

She gasped, ''But that's treason!''

''Aye. What's more, we believe Prince John sent Dunstan on the Crusade precisely to ensure that Richard would never return. The problem was, we could never prove it. The best we could do was to convince Richard to send Dunstan back to England.''

''So that's why you hate him?''

Thomas turned his head away from her and stared out the open window at the slanting rays of the setting sun. The look on his face was unlike any she'd seen. After a long moment, he said, ''One of the men who didn't return from that ambush was my youngest brother, Edmund.''

''Oh, Thomas.'' Her heart ached for him, and at the same time, his words reminded her of how little she knew about him or his family.

He continued as if he had not heard her. ''Dunstan caused the death of a number of good men, and he might have been responsible for the death of our king if we hadn't stopped him.''

His entire demeanor had changed. In a way she was sorry she had pressed him for the details of his relationship with the baron, but as she thought about what he had just told her, she began to realize the significance of his admission.

Trying to keep her voice from revealing the distress she felt, she said, "So Baron Dunstan is your sworn enemy, and by making love to me, you could make sure that he would never have me, at least not as a virgin bride."

Thomas snapped his head around in surprise. "Dunstan had nothing to do with this." He grasped her shoulders and gave her a little shake. "He has nothing to do with *us*. I made love to you today because I have to leave, and I wanted you to understand the way I feel about you before I go."

The blood was rushing in her ears. "You wanted to put your mark on me before you ride off to join up with King Richard," she said dully. She reached down to pull the blanket around her. "Well, you've accomplished your goal. I'll not forget you, Thomas of Havilland. Even though I most likely will never see you again."

Thomas shook his head in exasperation. "What is it that has made you so unwilling to believe that a man might want you simply for yourself and no other reason? Of course you will see me again, you beautiful, stubborn wench. You're mine, remember? We belong together."

But Alyce was no longer hearing the words. The revelation about Thomas's hatred of Dunstan had smashed the tiny bud of hope she'd allowed to begin growing inside her. Her father had been right. It was best to be wary of all men. Her voice brittle, she said, "I think you'd better go."

Thomas's eyes were dark with worry. "I can't leave you like this, Alyce. You've got things all twisted in your head."

"I don't think so. I think I've finally got my head straight, perhaps for the first time since I met you. So go, Thomas. Go to your king and leave me and Sherborne in peace."

Scalding tears were building behind her eyes, but she refused to give in to them while Thomas could see her. He'd accomplished his goal. He'd kept her from Dunstan and had taken her as a prize for himself. Now he was in a hurry to be back with his men.

When he finally spoke, he sounded tired. "Sweetheart, you know that my men are waiting for me. If I stay here longer, it could endanger their lives as well as the king's."

She didn't look at him as she answered, "Aye, I've said that you should go."

"But you're angry with me, and I don't have the time to wait until your humor improves."

He made it sound as if she was a petulant child. "My humor will improve when I'm left alone," she answered.

He took her chin and turned her face toward him. "Then I'll go, but before I do, I want you to listen to me." He sounded like a commander in battle as he declared, "I love you, Alyce of Sherborne."

She swallowed painfully over the lump in her

throat. If he had started with those words instead of all the talk about Dunstan, would it have made a difference? She wanted to believe him, but the overwhelming feelings of tenderness and *trust* that she'd had when he'd held her in his arms were gone. They faced each other on the bed like two strangers.

"Go to your men, Thomas. I'll not be responsible a second time for putting them at risk."

He looked unhappy with her response, but he began to gather his clothes and get dressed.

"When Richard is free, I'll be back," he said tersely.

She made no reply.

Thomas finished dressing, his thoughts jumbled. How had things gone so wrong? He'd wanted to get everything clear with her before he left, to tell her and *show* her that he loved her. The showing part had gone fine, but he had the feeling that he'd botched the telling of it. For all the love ballads he crooned, it appeared that he was in sore want of lessons as to the fine points of the art of wooing.

He went to sit beside her again on the bed and tried to take her in his arms, but she pulled away. Desperate, he tried teasing. "Will you keep out of trouble until I can come back to claim you? You'll not go poisoning any wandering bands of knights or let yourself be thrown into any dungeons?"

He thought he detected the slightest softening of her mouth, but she didn't speak. "I may not be saying the words just right, because I've never said them to anyone before,'' he told her, ''but I do love you, Alyce Rose.''

She turned her face to look at him, her expression troubled. He was tempted to take her in his arms again and make love to her. When their bodies had been together, there had been perfect communication between them. It was only when words intervened that the trouble began.

He glanced out the window at the darkening sky. He couldn't delay, not even for another hour. He already was dangerously late in leaving for Dover.

''Will you kiss me goodbye?'' he asked softly.

Tears welled in her eyes and he realized that far from being hard and indifferent, Alyce was confused and hurt. Guilt stabbed at him. He'd thought their lovemaking would serve as a kind of promise that he would return to her, but he was afraid he'd been terribly wrong. Now he had no choice but to leave, carrying with him the memory of her tears.

He leaned toward her and brushed her lips briefly with his. ''I'll make this right, Alyce. Soon.''

Then he got up and walked quickly out of the room without looking back at her.

''Ah, Allie, luv. What did they do to ye at Dunstan Castle?'' Lettie asked, as she sat on the edge of the bed and took Alyce's hand. ''Ye've not eaten since ye got back. It's been two days now.''

Alyce moved to one side to make room for her nurse's ample posterior. "I told you, Lettie, we hardly slept on the way there and back."

"Aye, yer Sir Thomas looked like the walking death when he left last night. I don't know how he expected to ride all night long."

Alyce stiffened at the sound of his name. She'd spent most of the night shifting back and forth from hating Thomas to admitting that she was in love with him. She would remember the moments when his body had moved over hers, his mouth meltingly tender. Then she'd tell herself that he'd ridden back to Sherborne for the express purpose of claiming her before his enemy, Dunstan, could get the chance.

The story he'd told her was horrible. He had a right to hate the man whose treachery had resulted in his brother's death. But he had no right to use her as a method of revenge.

She gave Lettie's hand a squeeze. "Do you believe men ever really fall in love, Lettie?" she asked. "Or is it always mixed up with conquest or revenge or some baser desire?"

Lettie looked sad. "Ah, lass, I'm afraid yer father, may he rest in peace, turned ye into a cynic."

At that, Alyce sat up in bed. "Do you think it was love that made Philip of Dunstan get the prince to promise me in marriage? He'd never even laid eyes on me."

"Aye, 'tis harder for the rich and noble. Sometimes I think the simple village folk have an easier time in matters of the heart.''

Alyce lay back on the bed. ''I wish I were a simple villager then, Lettie.''

''So ye could trust yer heart when it tells ye that ye've fallen in love with Sir Thomas?'' Lettie asked softly.

Alyce screwed her face into a scowl. ''No. So I could live out my life happily by myself and never have to worry about another man making me unhappy.''

Chapter Ten

It had been six weeks since Thomas's departure, and the doubts Alyce had had were gone. For all his sweet words of love, Thomas Havilland had been no different than all the other men her father had driven away while he'd still been around to protect her. As the weeks passed with no word from him, she tucked away the last bits of feeling that she'd let surface when the vibrant, handsome knight had ridden so unexpectedly into her life.

She had, however, two things for which to thank Thomas of Havilland. He had taken care of her problem with Prince John and Baron Dunstan. She'd heard nothing from either of them since her return from Dunstan Castle.

And he had convinced her once and for all that her father had been right to make her wary of all men. Now she knew the course she wanted for her life. She'd settle in and be a good mistress for all the people who loved her at Sherborne. Let the minstrels sing their ballads of love won and lost. She'd have a good, stable life with Lettie, Alfred, Fredrick and the others. They were her family, and it was all the happiness she needed.

Fredrick, whose father had been killed in an accident at the castle forge shortly after his son's birth, had been raised by his grandfather Alfred. It seemed natural to everyone at the castle, including Alyce, that as the old man grew increasingly frail, his grandson would take over many of his duties.

Fredrick's youthful enthusiasm proved a tonic for Alyce. He had many ideas about improvements for the castle and the surrounding farms, and Alyce was an eager listener. Together the two spent long days riding through the countryside during the daylight hours and poring over building plans at night by candlelight.

By the time two months had passed, her adventures with the Havilland knights seemed almost like a dream. Granted, it was a dream that sometimes returned to haunt her in the middle of the night, when she would awake in a sweat and remember the fevered kisses she and Thomas had shared. But, in general, she was able to put the whole episode out of her mind. Each day, as she and Fredrick planned some new improvement for Sherborne, her spirits lifted a little more.

She'd almost succeeded in convincing herself

that she was blissfully happy with her decision to spend the rest of her life unwed, hidden away at Sherborne.

"And at the Hartford Fair, milady," Fredrick was saying, as they stood on the castle wall surveying the nearby tenant farms, "they were advising that a field should lie fallow once every four years. That way the crops come in strong the next three."

Alyce wrinkled her nose. "Why? It would be hard to lose a full year's crops. Does it make sense to you?"

Fredrick pointed east, where neat plots of Sherborne land had been cleared generations ago, before the Normans ever came to England. "I don't know why, but I think it's worth the experiment. The barley has been weak and poor all along this stretch. I'd like to clear the land by the river so we'll have additional plots to give the tenants in order to leave these fields unplanted."

Fredrick couldn't read or write, but he had an innate intelligence and an instinct for the land that continually impressed Alyce. "Very well," she said. "We'll give it a try. And I'll see if I can find anything more on the subject in Father's books."

"I tried to talk with your father and my grandfather when I came back from the fair last year, but they were pretty set in their ways."

"Well, nothing's set anymore, so let's…" She

stopped suddenly and put her hand up to shade her eyes from the sun. "Look, riders."

Fredrick turned his head in the direction of her outstretched arm. "They're coming this way," he said.

Alyce squinted at the approaching horsemen, then looked at Fredrick, who met her gaze with worried eyes. "They carry the banner of Dunstan Castle," she said.

"Aye, and unless my eyes deceive me, milady, the tall one at the head of the procession is the baron himself."

He did not appear as evil and terrifying as he had when they were his prisoners back at Dunstan Castle. In fact, it appeared that Philip of Dunstan was taking some pains to impress Alyce with his affability.

After she and Fredrick had spotted the visitors from the castle wall, Alyce dashed back to her room to don the most regal robes she possessed, then had sat deliberately on her bed for half an hour so that the baron would be forced to wait for her. But when she finally descended to the great room, he rose to greet her with no sign of impatience.

"Lady Alyce," he said, his deep bass voice sounding almost silky, "at last we meet."

Once again, he was dressed all in red. Though he'd just come from the road, his robes were clean and fresh. His boots were scarlet leather without a speck of dust. Warily, she extended her hand and allowed him to bring it briefly to his lips. "You take us by surprise, Lord Dunstan. I wouldn't have expected to see you, since I no longer owe any obligation to the king or to Prince John. I paid the tax—"

He interrupted her. "I've not come to talk of obligation, milady, though your tax money never reached the prince, as I'm sure you must know."

At these last words, there was a subtle change in his black eyes that reminded Alyce once again of the man who had talked so easily about ripping out Fredrick's tongue. She suppressed a shiver and said firmly, "It was, nevertheless, delivered safely into your hands. I have witnesses to testify to that, if need be."

His smile was chilling. "I care nothing about witnesses." He gestured to the bench in front of the fireplace where he'd been waiting for her. "Shall we be seated?"

She had no desire to sit next to this man, who towered over her in his overwhelming crimson, but she took a seat on the far end of the bench. "Then perhaps you would state your business, Lord Dunstan, since I've had to interrupt some business I had with my steward regarding our tenant fields."

He sat in the middle of the bench and turned toward her. "You should not have to concern yourself with such matters, Lady Alyce. 'Tis not women's work. You need the guidance of a man to help you manage Sherborne.'' He looked around the big chamber as though trying to find something to prove that the castle was in dire need of a man's strong hand.

''It's nice of you to be concerned, but fortunately my father raised me precisely to deal with such matters. In the absence of a son, he wanted to be sure I had the training I needed to take care of Sherborne's welfare.''

''But surely he thought he would be around to manage it with you, and that you would have a husband's help before death ever took him from you. His untimely demise—''

She held up a hand. ''I've managed Sherborne for over a year now since his death. Forgive me for being rude, Baron, but I don't see how any of that should be your concern.''

He reached over and took her hand again. His fingers were ice-cold. ''I'll be honest with you, Lady Alyce. This past year, I've been quite busy with affairs of state. As you might imagine, Prince John has been terribly concerned about the plight of his brother. He has needed the support of his friends.''

Alyce felt she knew exactly the kind of concern Prince John had for his brother, but she refrained from making any comment.

''This has made me neglect you, my dear,'' Dunstan continued. ''And I apologize.''

That surprised her. "I've not felt neglected," she answered sharply. "On the contrary, I've been paid far too many visits for my liking. And now, if you'll excuse my directness once again, I'd really like nothing more than to be left alone."

The baron still held fast to her hand, in spite of her efforts to pull away. "The men who've visited you have obviously been idiots. They've paid for their ineptitude. Belatedly, I've realized that if I wanted this thing done right, I'd have to do it myself."

"This thing?" Alyce asked.

"Our betrothal. I've come to see it done myself."

Alyce yanked her hand from his grasp. "Then I'm sorry to tell you, Baron, that you've come for naught. I am not going to be betrothed to you or any other man."

His smile did not waver. "I understand that some women take a little coaxing, my dear Alyce. That is why, as I said, I've come myself this time."

She stood. "I'm not interested in being coaxed, Lord Dunstan. I'm sorry, but your visit here is to no purpose."

He stood as well, fully a head taller than she. "I'm a patient man, Lady Alyce, but not *too* patient. I'm prepared to give you a day or two to get used to my company."

Alyce looked around the room, and for the first time, she noticed that at every door to the great room there was a soldier wearing the Dunstan livery. All were fully armed.

"I'm under no obligation to you," she said. "You have no rights here at Sherborne."

He gave a little bow of his head. "As you said, milady, we surprised you. You may need a little time to get used to the idea. In the meantime—" he made a vague gesture around the room "—my men will take advantage of your hospitality."

From the far end of the hall, Fredrick was watching their conversation, a look of helplessness on his face. A few feet away from him, two of Dunstan's guards had seized Alfred and were holding his frail arms in an awkward position behind him. The old man grimaced against the pain.

Alyce felt hot and cold all at once. What should she do now? Somehow she had the feeling that Dunstan would not be chased away as easily as the messengers he had previously sent. She considered the rotten-meat trick, but discarded the idea. If he discovered what she had done, she had no doubt that the baron would take some kind of terrible revenge on the cooks and servants who carried out the deed.

She drew herself up as tall as she could. "Aye," she said stiffly, "I'd like some time."

"Very well," he said pleasantly. He motioned to one of his men. "The lady Alyce would like an escort to her chamber. Wait outside her door until she tells you that she'd like to talk with me again."

Alyce looked down to where the Dunstan guards still held Alfred. "If you want any hope of cooperation from me," she said, "you'll leave my people alone."

Dunstan followed the direction of her gaze. He gave a curt nod, and the two guards released their hold on the old man.

Satisfied for the moment, Alyce put her chin up and let the Dunstan guard lead the way out of the hall.

"It's just not the way I would have approached it, Thomas," Kenton said with a grin. It was a pleasant January evening and they'd decided to sleep outside, finding the cold air preferable to the crowded conditions inside the great hall of Nottingham Castle. King Richard, his ransom paid, had returned to England and had decided to stay at Nottingham through Easter. The building was full to the rafters. The great hall, where a number of Thomas's men had bunked down, reeked of sweat and smoke and the odor of men and clothes unwashed after months on the Continent.

Kenton and Thomas had bathed that morning. It was a habit Thomas had acquired as a boy at the insistence of his grandmother Ellen. When she had come from Normandy with the intention of "civilizing" the backward Saxons of Lyonsbridge, she'd ended up becoming more Saxon than Norman herself. But she'd upgraded the standards of cleanliness at the rambling old castle and had extended the neatness campaign to the people themselves.

His grandfather Connor sometimes grumbled that a yearly bath should be good enough for any soldier, but Thomas knew Connor himself often called for tubs of water to be brought to his chambers, especially those evenings when he and his wife had spent the entire dinner exchanging those special intimate glances that always had the rest of the Lyonsbridge household nodding in indulgent approval.

"From what I know of your lady Alyce, she's not one to respond well to being bullied," Kenton continued.

Thomas lay back on his bedroll and looked up at the stars. "Aye, but she didn't seem to respond well to my protestations of love, either."

"Perhaps you didn't know the right words to use," Kenton teased. "I could give you some lessons."

"Oh, could you now?"

"Aye. Are you forgetting that I always had three girls to your one when we were lads together at Lyonsbridge?"

"That was only because, being a decent sort, I *preferred* mine one at a time rather than in bunches."

Kenton laughed. "Well, I will admit that 'twas you who caught the fair Alyce's eye. She barely glanced at me, but as to these protestations of love, exactly how much time did you devote to them?''

''You know very well that I had to leave almost immediately to meet you and the men in Dover.''

Kenton lay back beside his friend and turned his gaze up to the sky as well. ''Did you tell her that her eyes sparkled like all the stars in the heavens?'' he asked, gesturing above him. ''That her skin was as soft as the petals of a flower? That her voice rivaled the lark in its melody?''

Thomas gave his friend a sardonic glance. ''Swounds, Kent, we only had a short time together. I wasn't going to waste it all on words.''

Kenton shook his head. ''That could be your mistake. Women need that kind of thing.''

''Alyce is not like that. She has more of a practical bent.''

''Ah, Thomas, all women need to be wooed, practical or no.''

Thomas gave a big sigh. ''I did my best, considering the limitations of time. She wasn't impressed.''

''Maybe she's not the one for you after all.''

Thomas stared straight up at the stars. ''Aye, she is. I'd stake my life on it, Kent.''

''It seems to me you already have. Or at least your happiness. You've gotten Richard to agree to grant you her hand in marriage. If it turns out to be a mistake, there will be no help for it.''

''It won't. She's just as much in love with me

as I am with her. All I need is some time to convince her of the fact.''

''And you think the way to do it is by having Richard's men drag her here and force her to marry you?''

''At least it will give me the time I need with her. In truth, Kenton, I can hardly sleep for thinking about her.''

Kenton stuffed a boot under his head for a pillow and rolled over. ''If you're so anxious to see her again, why didn't you go with the men Richard sent to fetch her?''

Thomas chuckled. ''I'm in love, Kenton, but I've not yet gone entirely crazy.'' Then he rolled to the opposite side and settled into his blankets, ready for one more night of restless sleep.

''So who has the king sent to fetch her?''

Thomas was silent for a moment. Finally he answered, ''Ranulf.''

Kenton sat bolt upright. ''Ranulf? And you let him go?''

Thomas grinned. ''Why not? 'Tis time my little brother gets a taste of the world.''

Lettie stood in the door frame, trying to use her solid, round form to block the tall man from entering the room. ''Milady is sleeping,'' she told him.

Philip of Dunstan glowered at the little woman. ''Move aside,'' he said. When Lettie stuck out her lip and refused to budge, he stepped back and motioned to two of his men, who were waiting just outside the door. In an instant they had each taken one of Lettie's arms, to carry her out of the room.

Dunstan stepped back across the threshold and approached the bed. In spite of Lettie's remark, Alyce had not been sleeping. She stood as he approached.

"You've had two days to think this over, Lady Alyce," he said politely. "And I have business elsewhere."

"Please feel free to go about your business, Baron. It's a waste of your time to stay here."

Dunstan paced from one side of her to the other, as if surveying a horse he intended to purchase.

"The fault may be mine," he said, still deceptively gracious. "Mayhap I didn't make myself clear enough. I came here to claim the bride that was promised to me by Prince John. I'll not leave until our betrothal has been made official."

Alyce shook her head, her chin up. "Then settle in for a long stay, milord. I have neither obligation nor desire to marry you."

He stopped directly in front of her, reached out a hand and put his long fingers around her neck. "Again, I haven't made myself clear. I'm not giving you a choice."

She felt the painful pressure of his thumb and finger under her ears, but she stood firm. "You can't force me into marriage. Even before I paid the tax, it was only the king or his regent who could do that.''

He leaned closer to her and increased the pressure on her neck. ''You might as well learn from the beginning, Alyce, my pet. I can do whatever I want where you're concerned. You're going to belong to me, body—'' he released her neck and ran his hand down her bodice, to take a rough hold on her breast ''—and soul.''

For a moment, Alyce thought she was going to be sick, but she swallowed down the nausea as she drew back her right hand and slapped the baron across the cheek as hard as she could.

Even as big as he was, the blow made him stagger. His eyes narrowed to dark points of fury. He shoved her back on the pallet, then bent over her, his knee on her stomach to hold her down.

''I don't mind a woman of spirit, Alyce. But understand this. That's the last time you'll ever hit me, unless you would like to see your kindly old nursemaid quartered and staked out to rot.''

The bile rose in Alyce's throat again. She looked around the room frantically for a weapon. There was a crockery pitcher sitting on the washstand. If she could just reach it...

Dunstan's knee dug into her stomach and his hands pinned her shoulders. Her arm couldn't quite cover the distance to the pitcher. She tried to distract him with more argument. ''We may be missing a king, but there is still a rule of law in England. I can't believe that even Prince John will condone you taking me by threats and force.''

''Prince John will condone what I tell him to—'' Dunstan began, but before he could finish, one of his soldiers burst into the room.

Dunstan turned on the man, his expression thunderous. ''What do you want?'' he roared.

''I beg your pardon, my liege,'' the man said, shaking. ''I thought you should know that a contingent of soldiers has just entered the gates. They've come from King Richard.''

Dunstan looked startled. ''From Prince John, you mean.''

The man shook his head vigorously. ''No, milord. From Richard. He's back. King Richard has returned to England.''

Chapter Eleven

It had taken less than an hour for Dunstan to gather his men and ride out of Sherborne. The stunning news of Richard's return had made the baron lose all interest in thoughts of betrothals.

Furiously, he'd questioned the young knight who'd brought the word. Richard's man didn't seem the least intimidated by the older man's wrath. Calmly, he'd explained that Richard had been ransomed and had returned to England to re-establish his crown. He was staying in Nottingham through the Easter holidays.

Dunstan had scarcely glanced at Alyce as he'd ordered his men to prepare to ride immediately to Prince John to warn him of the king's return.

Alyce had watched them go with relief. Without the timely interruption of King Richard's emissary, she wasn't sure what her fate might have been. But thoughts of Dunstan faded as she stood opposite the young man who had come from Richard, her mouth gaping open in astonishment. Twice she'd asked the man to repeat the message he'd brought to her, and still she could not believe it.

"I've paid a tax to buy my freedom from my feudal obligation to the king," she said, though she knew that it would do her little good to argue with this man, who obviously had no authority to do anything other than follow his orders.

"Aye, milady," the young knight said agreeably. "So you've explained, but my orders are to fetch you back to Nottingham, where the king awaits your pleasure."

Alyce went up on her tiptoes trying to keep the fury from exploding out the top of her head. "My *pleasure* would be to have nothing to do with the king or this new bridegroom he has picked out for me. Who is the man, anyway?"

"'Tis one of the king's closest supporters, milady."

"Does he have a name?"

"Aye, Thomas. Sir Thomas Brand."

Another Thomas, she thought grimly. Just to add to the aggravation.

"And what do they call you?"

"Ranulf, milady."

"Well, Sir Ranulf, you can tell your king and his Sir Thomas that I refuse their kind offer of helping me with my plans for the future. From now on, I intend to take care of myself."

The slender young knight was sharper than she gave him credit for. Respectfully, not meeting her gaze too directly, he asked, "Is that what you were doing with Lord Dunstan, milady? Planning for your future?"

She couldn't deny that Richard's troops had come at a fortuitous time. It was astute of Ranulf to point out that to all appearances she had *not* been doing a very good job of taking care of herself when they arrived. But she spoke firmly. "As you no doubt have guessed, Baron Dunstan was no more a welcome guest here than you. But I would have found a way to deal with him if your arrival had not driven him away." She was not as sure of this as she sounded, but Dunstan was no longer an immediate threat, whereas this man was.

"I'm sure you would, milady. I've been told of your…er…skill at dealing with visitors."

Alyce flushed. Who knew what tales they were telling of her at court? She studied the man, who stood before her patiently, with no sign of agitation. If they knew she was difficult to deal with, they must have had confidence in this Ranulf or they'd not have sent him. He was a pleasant-looking man, slender, but with broad shoulders and handsome features. Something about him appeared familiar, but she couldn't decide what it was.

"If they told you about me, weren't you afraid to come?"

Ranulf flashed a grin, and at that moment she

realized what had seemed familiar. "Sir Ranulf, your surname is not Havilland?"

"Nay, milady," he answered, and did not offer anything further.

She sighed. "What are your orders if I refuse to go with you?"

"My only orders are to bring you, milady. The means were left to my discretion."

He was nowhere near as big or as menacing as Dunstan, but she had the feeling that Sir Ranulf was capable of throwing her on the back of a horse and keeping her tied there all the way to Nottingham if she resisted.

Thomas had said that, unlike Prince John, King Richard was an honorable man. Perhaps her best chance lay in going to see the king herself to plead her case.

"Tell me, Sir Ranulf," she asked, "do you consider Richard to be a fair king? You may speak freely. No one is here to report your words."

Ranulf smiled at her, and once again his expression carried a haunting resemblance to Thomas Havilland. "Aye, milady. Richard is a fair king and a good man."

"Then I'll go with you peacefully. I'd like to get this matter settled once and for all before the road to Sherborne is worn into trenches by foolish men riding back and forth trying to meddle in my life."

* * *

Nottingham Castle was the grandest place Alyce had ever seen. Within the thick walls of the castle grounds were a number of buildings, centering around a magnificent keep that had stood since the days of the Conquerer.

Ranulf escorted her inside with his usual courtesy. His company had proven surprisingly agreeable on the two-day ride. She didn't know if it was his youthful self-confidence or his odd resemblance to Thomas, but she felt immediately comfortable with him. His good humor helped her forget for long moments the reason they were riding toward Nottingham.

The trip would have been made more quickly if Alyce hadn't insisted that Lettie accompany her. Without a complaint, Ranulf had arranged for a litter to carry the older woman, and had slowed the pace of the journey accordingly.

As they rode across the courtyard to the stables, Alyce admitted to herself that she had some curiosity about seeing the great King Richard—the Lion Heart, they'd begun to call him after his valiant rescue of the beleaguered Christian stronghold at Jaffa. "Has the king recovered from his wounds?" she asked Ranulf.

"Aye, milady," the young knight replied. He helped her dismount and handed the reins of their horses to a stable boy. "He's hale and hearty again. 'Tis unfortunate, some say."

"Unfortunate?"

"Because he's already talking about leading another Crusade."

"Perhaps I'll be lucky and my new bridegroom will go with him," Alyce said with a grimace.

"I'd not count on it, milady," Ranulf said dryly.

They stood waiting as Lettie's litter rumbled up. The nurse climbed out, stretching her back and moaning at the jouncing ride.

"We'll get you to a bed, Lettie dear," Alyce said.

The older woman shook her head and waved her hand back and forth at the couple as though shooing away a fly. "Go on, Allie, go on ahead. I'm fine, and I won't be leaving here until I see that our things are unloaded properly."

With an amused smile at how the round little woman set the stable boys to scurrying around, Ranulf offered his arm to escort Alyce across the littered yard of the bailey. "I don't think you'll be as disappointed with your future husband as you expect, milady," he said as they started walking toward the door to the main keep. "He's a very well-favored man."

Curious in spite of herself, she asked, "What does he look like?"

There was an impish glint in Ranulf's eyes. "There's a certain family resemblance among all the Brand brothers."

"He has brothers?"

"Aye, two. Though one is still missing in the Holy Lands." A shadow crossed his face.

"A family resemblance won't help me, Ranulf, since I've never made the acquaintance of any of the Brands."

"Aye, milady, you have." They'd almost reached the door when he stopped walking and gave a little bow. "Ranulf Brand, at your service."

Alyce drew back, astonished. "His brother?"

"Aye, Lady Alyce. Sir Thomas is my big brother." Then he grasped her shoulders and pulled her toward him for a perfunctory kiss on each cheek. "Welcome to Nottingham, sister-in-law."

She was just recovering from her surprise when the huge door of the castle slammed open and a familiar voice shouted angrily, "I told you to bring her safely, you blackguard, not to put your meaty paws on her."

Ranulf turned toward the newcomer without alarm, a grin on his face. "I'm merely giving your bride a proper welcome to the city, Thomas, since you weren't around to perform the task."

His bride? Alyce gaped at the two men. Her prospective bridegroom, Thomas *Brand,* was none other than her former lover, Thomas *Havilland?*

"Why didn't you tell me?" she asked Ranulf, indignant and a little hurt. She had liked the affable young knight. Now she could add him to the list of men who had in some way betrayed her.

Ranulf gave her an apologetic smile. "Thomas wasn't sure you'd come if you knew whom you were about to marry." He shrugged and gave Thomas a teasing glance. "I didn't understand it, frankly. My brother here is normally a supremely cocky rascal, but it seems he's met his match in you, Lady Alyce. You have him breaking out in nervous sweats and—"

Thomas bounded down the remaining two stairs and gave his brother a not-too-friendly punch on the arm. "That'll be enough, little brother. You've finished your job, and I can take over the welcoming duties from here on."

The punch stopped Ranulf's words but didn't alter his teasing smile.

Alyce turned her anger on Thomas. "It was cruel of you to make me come here thinking I was to marry a stranger."

"Would you have come along more willingly if they'd told you that your bridegroom was the knight you knew as Thomas Havilland?" he asked.

She would have come more willingly if the said Thomas Havilland had come to her himself, explained his absence and told her again the words she'd heard him say just before he'd left her at Sherborne. Shouldn't that be as logical to a man as it was to her? Though, to be fair, when he had declared his love to her, she hadn't given him any encouragement.

She studied him, taking her time with an answer.

He looked older than he had three months ago. She didn't remember the lines etched alongside his mouth. Or perhaps it was just that she'd spent two days looking at his younger brother. Seeing them together, the resemblance was more obvious. She should have guessed the relationship immediately.

Ranulf and Thomas were waiting for her reply. "No woman wants to be forced into a marriage— any marriage," she said.

Thomas looked as if her answer was what he had expected. "But you came, nevertheless," he said.

"I was given no choice," she said, glancing at Ranulf.

"I've only just now taken the chains off her hands and feet," Ranulf teased.

Neither Thomas nor Alyce were in the mood for humor. "The king felt that you would be better off with the protection of a husband, especially considering Dunstan's interest in you," Thomas said.

"In fact, we had to chase your friend the baron off when we arrived."

Thomas looked at his brother in astonishment. "Dunstan was there? At Sherborne?" He turned to Alyce for an explanation.

She spoke sarcastically. "Evidently the baron had the same idea as you—that I needed protection. The only difference is that he felt *he* should be the chosen one."

Thomas moved a step closer to her and spoke in

a low voice. "How long was he there? Did he hurt you?"

Alyce glanced briefly at Ranulf, then decided she didn't care if Thomas's brother heard her words. "If you mean did he have his way with me, no, your brother's arrival prevented that."

There was a noticeable relaxing of Thomas's shoulders. "Thank God. Did Dunstan offer you any resistance?" he asked Ranulf. He didn't seem surprised that his slender younger brother had evidently had little trouble in chasing away an opponent as formidable as the baron.

"Nay. Unfortunately, the bastard made no effort to fight us. I think he was too astonished to hear that Richard was back, especially after everything he and John did to prevent that from ever occurring. All he wanted to do was ride with the news to the prince."

Thomas turned to Alyce. "You may not like my tactics, Alyce, but believe me, 'tis for the best. Richard is already talking of leaving the country again. Once he's gone, you'd be at the mercy of Prince John and Dunstan."

"Unless I have a husband to protect me."

"Aye," he said firmly.

They glared at each other.

"Well, then," Ranulf said briskly, dusting his hands together. "Now that I have reunited you two lovebirds, I'll just be off to find myself a flagon of ale and some friendly companionship. I've enjoyed traveling with you, milady," he added to Alyce.

She turned her gaze from Thomas to Ranulf and offered him a smile. "Aye, thank you for your courtesy, Ranulf, and for your patience with Lettie."

"Ah, milady, now there I had no choice," he said with a wink. "From the fiery look in your maid's eyes, I was afraid she would have emasculated me if I'd refused to take her along to protect you."

The woman in question was coming toward them as they spoke, directing two hapless servants who were loaded down with bags and trunks. "Careful not to drag anything in the dirt," she ordered. "I'll not have my lady meeting the king in muddy rags."

Ranulf and Alyce exchanged a smile. "All the same," she said softly, extending her hand, "I'm grateful."

"I thought you were leaving, Ranulf," Thomas said pointedly. He seemed irritated by the fact that Alyce had a smile for his brother, but not for him.

"I wouldn't mind some ale, as well," Alyce said to Ranulf.

Ranulf gave his brother a helpless shrug, but couldn't resist a grin as he took Alyce's hand and placed it on his arm. "Then we'll go together to find some, milady. We need to wash off the dust

of the road.'' Over his shoulder he said carelessly,
''You may join us if you care to, Thomas.''

Thomas slapped the side of his thigh in frustration, then turned to follow them through the big
castle doors.

''Ye sent for me, Sir Thomas?'' Lettie's tone
was wary.

Thomas stood as the little woman entered the
small solar where he'd been waiting for her. He
motioned for her to sit down. She did so stiffly,
obviously uncomfortable with this breach of mas-
ter-servant protocol. ''Aye, I wanted to speak with
you,'' he said.

Her chin went up. Thomas smiled. Now he knew
from whom Alyce had picked up that particular
gesture of defiance.

''I'll not speak a word against my mistress, Sir
Thomas, so don't be expecting it of me.'' Then she
proceeded to let the words pour out. ''She can be
stubborn, aye, it's true, but only because she's had
nothing but people trying to push her around, one
way or t'other, ever since her father's death. Deep
down, she's as soft as they come, a loving, caring
girl with a heart as big as—''

Thomas held up a hand to interrupt her. ''You'll
get no argument from me, Lettie. I not only admire
your mistress, I'm in love with her.''

The nurse's gray eyes widened. ''Ye are?'' she
asked.

"Aye. I have been ever since I first laid eyes on her, just after you and she connived to poison my men."

Lettie flushed. "'Twas pure desperation, milord. She'd been sorely tested, you see, what with all those men coming and going, telling her what to do—"

He interrupted her again. "I'm not blaming her, Lettie, nor you. You were all defending your home, in a manner of speaking."

The old woman looked relieved, but a little confused. "Beggin' yer pardon, Sir Thomas, but if ye claim to be in love with the lass, why have ye forced her to come here?"

"Because I want to marry her, and I wasn't sure if she'd have me."

Lettie shook her head in disgust. "So of course the most logical thing to make her *want* to marry ye would be to drag her clear across England, against her will..." She crossed her arms over her ample breasts and pinned Thomas with a scolding gaze. "Why is it that men in love seem to have the brainpower of a pea?"

Thomas gave a rueful laugh. "I don't know, Lettie. I've asked myself the same question. So you think it was a mistake to bring her here?"

"Aye," she answered firmly.

"When I told her back at Sherborne that I loved her, before I left to join Richard, she didn't want to have anything to do with me."

Lettie's face softened. "Ah, young man, sometimes women want a little bit of coaxing. *Coaxing,*" she added forcefully, "not *dragging*. Unfortunately, Alyce may need more than most, thanks to all the nonsense Lord Sherborne planted in her head."

"Her father?"

"Aye, he spent her whole life convincing her that the only reason a man would ever want her would be to take over Sherborne Castle."

"Surely one glance in the looking glass would convince her otherwise?"

"Nay. She thinks the only reason men want to marry her is for Sherborne alone."

"Sherborne is a modest holding," Thomas observed. The Lyonsbridge fortune could buy Sherborne ten times over, but he didn't mention that to the maid, who looked a little insulted at his characterization of her home.

"It may be modest, but it's all Alyce has ever known, and she's not about to let some man take it away from her."

Thomas sighed. "Philip of Dunstan was far wealthier than she. He may have wanted Sherborne, but he wanted the lady Alyce as well."

"That's not the way my lady saw it."

The room grew quiet as Thomas sat lost in thought. "Was there anything more, Sir Thomas?" Lettie asked finally.

"What would it take to convince her that a man might love her for herself alone?" he asked.

"Ah, milord," Lettie said, standing, "ye'd best go back to yer minstrel love ballads if ye want the answer to that question." Then she bobbed a curtsy and turned to leave the room.

"Ye could hear him out, Allie luv," Lettie said, fussing with her charge's hair. They had pulled the honey-colored locks up onto her head with a pearl circlet in preparation for her audience with King Richard.

"I have heard him out, Lettie. I find him no different than any other man."

"Ye've never deceived me before, Alyce Rose. But I think ye're doing it now. Either that or ye're deceiving yerself."

Alyce gave a little shriek as Lettie tugged an errant strand into place. "I'm not deceiving anyone, Lettie. He's more agreeable than Dunstan, I'll grant you that. But he's the one who has been deceiving. He didn't even tell me his real name. And he's had me brought here for marriage as though I were some kind of chattel."

Lettie spoke softly. "I think he loves ye, Allie."

Alyce spoke sharply. "What does that mean? He wants me in his bed? Aye, I have no doubt of that. He wants to be master of Sherborne? Aye, that, too. What else is love, Lettie? Can you tell me?"

Her eyes filled with tears as she turned to her

nurse to ask the question. Lettie shook her head sadly. "I'm hoping the day will come when ye find out, lass," she said.

They both turned toward the door at the sound of a knock. Lettie crossed over and opened it. The visitor had the uniform of a royal page.

"Good day, mistress, milady," he said, bowing at the waist. "I've come to fetch you. King Richard awaits your attendance."

Chapter Twelve

Even in the isolation of Sherborne, Alyce had heard tales of the great King Richard. The accounts told of how he himself had led the assault, wading ashore at the head of troops, to relieve the garrison at Jaffa. He was a fierce, sometimes cruel warrior. Yet he was also the darling of the troubadours, having written the lyrics for many of their ballads.

The serving maid who had been assigned to her and Lettie in the crammed castle told them that after the Easter holidays the king was planning to head back to the Continent to see to his holdings there and the possibility of another Crusade.

Alyce wondered how the monarch had managed to find the time during his short stay to pay attention to the affairs of Sherborne, which surely must be one of his very minor holdings. Undoubtedly, she would not have merited the king's attention without Thomas's prompting. She sighed. If it hadn't been for Richard and Thomas, she reminded herself, she'd have Prince John and Dunstan to contend with.

She tried to make her pace stately as she approached the hall that the king had adopted for his receiving room during his stay. She knew that Lettie, walking alongside her, was watching her with a critical eye, hoping that for once her charge would behave with proper decorum.

Even if she'd wanted to take a little skip to relieve the tension, Alice probably wouldn't have been able to in her heavy costume. Over the thick fustian cloth of her undergown she wore a cloth-of-gold tunic that had belonged to her mother. She'd looked at it many times when Lettie had tenderly taken out the garment to air, but she'd never dared put it on. When they'd left Sherborne, Lettie had insisted on packing the beautiful piece, declaring that it was the only thing in Alyce's wardrobe truly fit to wear in a king's company.

The receiving room was full of people, mostly men. Alyce's gaze went immediately to Thomas, who was standing near the front of the room, talking with a man of about his own height. Even at a distance, she recognized the thick chestnut hair and regal bearing of the man called Lion Heart.

His features were handsome, but there was little humor or warmth in his face. Her knees shook slightly as the crowd parted to give her room to approach. Lettie fell behind, leaving Alyce to make the walk by herself.

She spotted Thomas's lieutenant, Kenton, in the throng, and then Ranulf, who gave her an encouraging smile and a wink. Drawing herself up and trying not to feel the weight of the tunic dragging at her shoulders, she marched straight to the front of the room. When she'd reached the king, she sank low in a curtsy that she and Lettie had secretly practiced the previous evening.

"Your majesty, may I present Lady Alyce of Sherborne?" Thomas said. He extended his hand toward her and she found herself clinging to it as she rose to her feet. When she was standing straight, he kept hold of her, and she didn't pull away. His hand was warm and solid, and it gave her courage as she faced the king.

Her appearance seemed to make little impression on Richard. He gave her a brief glance, nodded, then turned to one of his courtiers to begin a conversation on another matter. Alyce stood bewildered. This was the man who by rule of law and sovereignty had total power over the course of her life, yet he gave her no more attention than if she had been a mouse dashing across the floor.

Thomas seemed to sense her confusion. He leaned close to her and whispered, "The king has many things on his mind today."

"And obviously I am not one of them," she said, not bothering to lower her voice.

The sound drew Richard's attention. He turned back to her. "Lady Sherborne, is Sir Thomas attending to your needs?"

"I have no particular needs at the moment, your majesty," Alyce answered. Some distance behind her, she could hear Lettie give a distressed cough.

Richard didn't seem to have heard her. His eyes were on Thomas. "I see why you wanted her, Thomas," he said. "She's a pretty thing."

Thomas gave Alyce an apologetic glance, but answered respectfully, "Aye, your majesty. Lady Alyce is as lovely as she is intelligent. You've made me a fortunate man."

"I owed you, Thomas." His gaze flickered to Alyce, then back to Thomas. "And I pay my debts. Remember that the next time I ask for a favor."

"I shall, your majesty," he replied with a slight bow.

Richard appeared done with the audience and ready to move on. She'd been dealt with as summarily as a troublesome servant, Alyce thought, her anger rising. Granted, Sherborne was a tiny place, probably unworthy of much of the king's attention, but no matter how small, he was its feudal lord. By law, she owed him allegiance and he owed *her* protection.

"Your majesty," she said loudly. Out of the corner of her eye, she could see Thomas wince. "I'd like to speak to you about this marriage that you've proposed for me."

The king turned back to her, surprised. For the first time, he focused all the power of his deep blue eyes on her face, and she suddenly understood why he'd been able to inspire loyalty among his soldiers and hatred among his enemies.

"Your marriage? What do you have to say about it, Lady Sherborne?" he asked softly.

It seemed as if the entire room had gone deathly quiet. Even the rustling of the silken robes of the numerous clerics had ceased. Alyce cleared her throat. "I have no desire to be married," she said.

There was no change in Richard's expression, but his eyes looked at her with deeper interest. "Indeed?" He looked at Thomas. "I'd thought you said that the lady of Sherborne had already expressed an interest."

Thomas shook his head. "If you remember correctly, your majesty, I said that I was the one who was interested. I was unsure of the lady's feelings."

Richard's thick eyebrows went up. "Do you have some objection to Sir Thomas?" he asked Alyce.

"Nay, that is—" she stumbled for the words "—I don't object to him precisely, but to the idea of being forced to marry any man."

For the first time, there was a touch of warmth in the king's face and he appeared to almost smile. "You prefer to manage Sherborne Castle all by yourself?" he asked.

She nodded.

He turned to Thomas. "I'm not particularly in favor of forcing my subjects into marriages they oppose, Thomas. I hadn't realized that your lady was unwilling. Perhaps we need to reconsider the idea."

Alyce felt a surge of triumph, coupled with a totally unexpected twinge of disappointment. She hadn't really thought that the king would listen to her plea to be let out of the match, so she hadn't taken the time to analyze how she would feel about it if he actually set her free, to ride back to Sherborne an independent woman. And never see Thomas Brand again.

But Thomas was speaking. "I beg your pardon, your majesty, but I believe it's imperative for this marriage to be carried out immediately."

"Why's that?"

Thomas looked around and picked Ranulf out of the crowd. "Tell the king who was at Sherborne when you arrived," he told his brother.

Ranulf took a step forward. "Baron Dunstan was there with a number of his men."

Richard's face darkened. He looked at Alyce. "My brother's choice for you, I believe?"

Alyce felt her brief flirtation with freedom vanishing. "The baron was an unwelcome visitor. My people and I would have dealt with him," she said. She waited for Ranulf to speak up and reveal exactly how entrenched the Dunstan troops had been when he arrived, but he remained silent.

"The lady doesn't seem to fear Dunstan, Thomas. Is he the only reason you request an immediate marriage?" the king asked.

Thomas looked from the king to Alyce, obviously feeling that his case was weakening. He took a deep breath and said, "Might I speak with you in private a moment, your majesty?"

Richard looked surprised, but he nodded. He made a slight gesture with his hand, and all at once the men who had been surrounding him started to back away, giving him space to speak to Thomas without being overheard. One of the courtiers took Alyce gently by the elbow and pulled her back as well.

"So, Thomas," Richard said, when everyone was safely out of earshot. "Tell me why I should give you the lady Alyce when she professes to be unwilling."

"I do believe Dunstan to be a threat to her, your majesty, in spite of what she says. There's that and then—" he took a deep breath "—there's the fact that Lady Alyce might already be carrying my child."

The king's eyebrows rose. "I see," he said slowly, then added, "You are aware that she is under my protection?"

Thomas's gaze did not falter. "Aye, your majesty."

"I take it the lady *was* willing in this, at least."

"As you know me, your majesty, you know that I would never take to my bed a woman who was unwilling."

Richard was silent for a long moment. "Aye, Thomas, I believe you. But if she was willing then, why is she objecting to the marriage now?"

Thomas gave a sigh of exasperation. "I'm not sure, your majesty, but I suspect it's because she's made up her mind that she should be independent."

The corner of Richard's mouth quirked. "Are you quite sure you want such a woman to wife, Thomas?"

"Aye, your majesty."

The king glanced over at Alyce, who was watching the two men intently from some distance away. "From what you say, she might be happier if you wait and, er, *court* her a bit."

"Aye, but in the meantime she may have Dunstan to contend with, and I'd not take that risk."

Richard gave a nod of approval. "Then under the circumstances, the betrothal shall be this afternoon. The bishop of Westminster will perform the ceremony."

He motioned for his courtiers to approach, then signaled to one of the scarlet-robed clerics. "Your grace, I'd appreciate it if you would make yourself available this afternoon to perform a betrothal," he said.

"Certainly, my lord," the bishop murmured.

"The castle is crowded," Richard said to Thomas. "I'll direct that you be given special lodgings for your betrothal night."

"Thank you, your majesty," Thomas said with a bow.

Alyce had not even been consulted. She stepped forward, ready to argue her case anew, but Richard merely raised his hand and said, "I'm giving you into the hands of a fine man, Lady Sherborne. May your union be long and blessed." Then he turned away, his attention already moving on to other matters.

It had happened so fast. A betrothal was not as final as a marriage, but the vows were sacred, given before the eyes of God as manifested on earth by the bored bishop of Westminster, who was obviously annoyed to have his afternoon nap disrupted by such an unimportant event.

She wore the cloth-of-gold tunic and pearls, and Lettie fussed over her and cried, while Alyce stood dazed and unbelieving. By sundown she was betrothed, seated next to her bridegroom at King Richard's long table, sharing a trencher with Thomas, picking at the succulent pieces of meat he cut for her, tasting nothing.

They lingered at the meal only long enough to be polite. It had been decided that the newly betrothed couple would be given the privacy of a

small guardhouse located at one corner of the castle walls. Thomas had accepted the offer with a
terse thank-you. He'd shaken off the congratula-
tions and ribald comments of his men, and had
scarcely spoken to either Kenton or Ranulf, both
of whom watched with worried expressions as the
betrothed couple made their way out of the hall.

"I'm afraid my brother's made a mistake to
force her like this," Ranulf said. He and Kenton
held out their mugs as a serving maid passed with
a pitcher of ale.

"He thought he had no choice," Kenton said.
"Richard is set on leaving again within the month,
and then she'd be in danger from Prince John."

Ranulf nodded gloomily over his ale. "Aye, but
she looked so unhappy. It will take some convincing to get her to see the sense of it."

Their gazes went to the door of the hall through
which Alyce and Thomas had exited. "Perhaps it
will work itself out. Your brother can be convincing," Kenton said.

"Aye, I know. But first the lady has to be willing to listen to what he has to say."

Kenton smiled. "You're young yet, Ranulf. If
Thomas is wise, the kind of convincing he'll use
has little to do with words."

The early spring twilight was getting longer each
day, and there was still a band of light in the western sky as Alyce and Thomas walked out of the

main keep and over to the little stone house. Neither spoke, and the short distance across the courtyard seemed to take forever.

During supper, Thomas had attempted to make conversation, but when her answers had been short and distant, he had stopped talking. They'd left without ceremony. She hadn't even said goodbye to Lettie.

"This is it," Thomas said, breaking the evening stillness. He opened the latch of the wooden door. "I trust it will be satisfactory. Lettie said that she had brought over some of your..." he hesitated "...ah, personal things."

Alyce smiled. Though Thomas had faced the fiercest warriors in battle without a qualm, he looked as if the world of female possessions was a mystery he did not care to probe. The idea eased some of the tension that had been building in her since the audience with Richard that morning. Her back and neck were stiff with it.

The truth was, she admitted to herself as she walked into the little guardhouse, she was no longer sure what she wanted. For the past year, thinking that her fate might be to marry Baron Dunstan, she'd sworn that if she were forced to marry, she'd make sure that her husband would rue the day he had taken the vows.

But suddenly it was not an old, evil man who was taking her to her bridal bed, but Thomas, the man who had kissed a serving girl named Rose and changed her forever.

The guardhouse was simple, with a fireplace, already lit, at one end, plus a small table and chairs. A generous bed was made up with fresh linens; on the small nightstand next to it was a jug and two tumblers.

She walked over to the fire and stretched out her hands. The heat felt good on her palms, but did nothing to warm the chill she had inside. She felt more confused and alone than she had since the days just after her father's death.

Thomas came up behind her. "Would you like some wine?" he asked.

She shook her head.

He moved around her toward the fire. "There's a chill in here. I'll build this up."

She stood stock-still as he threw several more small logs on the blaze, brushed off his hands and stood, studying her frozen expression.

"Are you tired, sweetheart?" he asked.

She stiffened at the endearment. His voice had the same husky tones she remembered from the afternoon they had made love at Sherborne. Against her will, she could feel the slow uncurling of her senses.

She shook her head and continued staring at the fire.

Behind her, Thomas gave a sigh. "My stubborn

little Rose. What do I have to do to win a smile from you? Or at least a word?''

She remained silent.

He moved closer and put his hands on her shoulders. ''You looked so beautiful today,'' he murmured. ''I vow I was the envy of every man at the castle.''

A single tear made its way down her cheek and glistened in the firelight. He saw it and turned her around in his arms, clasping her against him. ''Ah, sweetheart, don't cry. How can I make this easier for you? You've not given up your independence, my fierce Alyce. You've merely gained an ally to stand with you in confronting the world.''

His words were convincing, but she wasn't yet ready to succumb to the comforting vision they painted. The tears began streaming down both cheeks. She ignored them and kept her voice hard as she answered, ''Allies are equals who *choose* to unite themselves against a common foe. You and I are conquerer and vanquished. Words will not alter the facts.''

His hands dropped from her arms. ''Was that the way you felt when we made love at Sherborne? Like conquerer and vanquished?''

She looked up into his eyes. ''Nay, for that was a union of equals.''

He traced the trail of her tears with his thumb. ''I didn't do this to make you unhappy,'' he said. ''I did it to keep you safe. Would you rather be back at Sherborne fighting off Dunstan right now?''

She gave a watery smile. "At least he's an easy enemy to hate.''

Thomas immediately seized on the small advantage she'd given him. "Which means I am not?'' he asked.

She gave a small, reluctant shake of her head.

His smile was relieved. "Perhaps you can't hate me because you know, deep down, that I'm not your enemy at all.'' He put his hand at the back of her neck, then bent to kiss her gently. "Enemies rarely kiss,'' he whispered.

She steeled herself not to respond to the touch of his lips. His smile faded. "I know you haven't forgotten what we had together,'' he said. "Why should it be different, just because a priest has read some words over us?''

Aye, the priest had said words binding them together. She wondered if Thomas would ever understand how she had felt that afternoon, surrounded by strangers, men who were determined to steer the course of her life. She'd thought of her father, who had always depended on his daughter to be as strong as a son. No son of Sherborne would have been sold in matrimony.

Her tears stopped flowing. All at once she felt tremendously tired. "You're not my enemy, Thomas, but neither will I welcome you to my bed.

You've forced me to a betrothal, but you can't force me to respond to your lovemaking.''

A flash of anger flared in his eyes. "Would you deny us both what we want because I didn't have time to ride weekly to Sherborne for months on end to court you with pretty words and sonnets?''

She shook her head. ''You've made a poor bargain, Thomas. 'Twas only a betrothal. No wedding vows were spoken. Perhaps it's not too late for you to change your mind and tell the king you want a more amenable bride.''

His mouth tightened. ''Thank you for the advice, milady, but I'll not be taking it. You see, unlike you, I do know what I want.''

His anger was easier to face than the earlier tenderness. She tilted up her chin and glared at him. ''Good for you, Sir Thomas. That makes you a rare and fortunate man, but it doesn't change my mind. If you want me in your bed this night, I'll be brought there against my will, just as I was to the altar this afternoon.''

She could see his hands flexing at his sides, as if he wished he could shake some sense into her, but she stood without flinching.

''I've never forced a woman to my bed,'' he said stiffly. ''And I'm not about to start with you.'' Then he spun around and stalked out of the building.

Alyce stood awkwardly in the center of the room after he left, expecting him to return at any moment. When several minutes passed with no sign of him, she relaxed her shoulders and let out a long stream of air. Now what? She couldn't imagine where he had gone when everyone in the castle expected that they were in their betrothal bed together.

She looked around the room, trying to decide what she should do. She could go back to the castle, but the place was so full it was possible that they had given away the pallet she'd been assigned the previous evening.

The fire burned brightly, lending a cozy glow to the place. Her body ached from too much standing throughout the day in the heavy gold tunic, and the fresh bed looked temptingly soft. Her betrothal bed.

With a grimace, she pulled the tunic over her head and threw it on the table. It was as if she'd shed the weight of the day along with it. Crooning a nearly tuneless ballad that had been a favorite of her father's, she crossed the room to the bed, curled up on it, pulled a blanket over herself and fell sound asleep.

Chapter Thirteen

Thomas paced back and forth along the thick old walls that still formed the defenses of Nottingham Castle. The noise of the after-dinner revelry drifted out from the main hall, but he hadn't wanted to return there. His presence would have caused gossip and ridicule. He was supposed to be enjoying the favors of his betrothed, not wandering about in the middle of the night like an unwelcome ghost.

For the tenth time, he reviewed in his head the conversation he had had with Alyce. He'd been so sure that once the troublesome legalities of their union were disposed of, she'd stop fighting him and admit that the two of them were destined to be together. Indeed, there had been moments in the guardhouse tonight when he'd thought her eyes had softened, when she'd seemed to respond to his warm voice and gentle touch.

But in the end she'd proven more implacable

than he would have imagined. Perhaps he'd been wrong in believing that her feelings matched his. Usually when a woman allowed a man to make love to her, it was because she was in love with that man. But Alyce was unlike any woman he'd ever known. With her taste for adventure, it was possible that she had joined in the lovemaking merely to satisfy her curiosity.

The question was what should he do now? The night air was chilly, though moist with the promise of spring. He'd hoped to spend that spring at Lyonsbridge, introducing his family to his new bride.

Footsteps sounded on the stone behind him. He whirled around, still accustomed to watching for enemies at every turn.

"Hold, Thomas, 'tis I." It was Kenton's voice, and in a moment his lieutenant drew near enough to be recognized in the darkness.

"Kenton. What are you doing here?" A kind of embarrassment at being caught out alone on the night of his betrothal made Thomas's tone harsher than he intended.

"I saw a figure walking up against the parapets and came to investigate. I hadn't expected it to be you."

The question was implied rather than asked, but Kenton was his oldest friend, and Thomas spoke frankly. "She turned me away. I'd thought after the ceremony she would give up her resentment, but I underestimated her stubbornness.''

Kenton was silent for a moment. Then he said, ''So you intend to wear a path in the flagstones all night long?''

Thomas's grin was sheepish. ''It's better than going back inside to admit that I've been sent away from my own betrothal bed.''

Kenton boosted himself up to perch on the edge of the wall. ''Come sit here. Your pacing is making me dizzy.''

Thomas complied. For several moments the two friends sat quietly on the wall, looking up at the few stars that blinked off and on in the cloudy skies.

''Mayhap it was a mistake,'' Thomas said finally.

Kenton clicked his teeth. ''I thought you said you loved the lady.''

''I did. I do, but if she's set against the marriage, 'twill serve no purpose but to make us both miserable.''

''Is this the warrior who held the flank at Jaffa, outnumbered three to one?''

''I'm beginning to think that was an easier battle to win,'' Thomas said grimly.

Kenton laughed. ''You'd rather face a thousand screaming Turks than one intrepid and fiery young woman.''

"Any day of the week," Thomas said forcefully.

"Ah, my friend, you disappoint me. I've never seen you give up so easily."

Thomas shrugged. "I haven't given up."

"It certainly looks like it. What did you tell her?"

"I didn't tell her anything. I just left."

Kenton rolled his eyes. "What did you tell her *before* you left? Did you take my advice about the pretty speeches?"

Thomas was silent, trying to remember. He had said she was beautiful, hadn't he? He was almost sure there'd been something about her being beautiful.

Kenton continued. "You did tell her that you loved her, didn't you? Surely you got that much right."

Had he told her that he loved her?

Kenton groaned with frustration.

Thomas felt sweat bead on his forehead. How could he not have told her that he loved her? he thought, furious at his own stupidity.

Kenton stood up. "You know what, Thomas? You deserve to be out here in the middle of the night freezing your tail instead of in a warm bed beside a soft woman. What's more, I wash my hands of the whole affair."

He gave Thomas a clap on the shoulder and walked away.

Thomas watched him go with a rueful smile. When he and Kenton had been growing up together, Thomas had always been the smart one. He was the leader on the battlefield and off. He was the one who was quick with sums, well read, savvy at court intrigues. But when it came to females, Kenton had always run circles around him.

Thomas pushed himself off the wall and straightened up. With luck, Alyce would still be there, waiting to give him another chance. His face set with purpose, he made his way back to the guardhouse.

The fire had burned down to embers by the time he returned, but there was enough light to tell him that Alyce was still there. She was not, however, waiting to give him another chance. From the soft rise and fall of her breathing underneath the blanket, she appeared to be in a deep and quite peaceful sleep.

Alyce awoke slowly. She couldn't remember the last time she'd slept so soundly. The sense of her surroundings came to her gradually, and with it she felt the contrast of the chilly air of the room with the warm body lying next to her.

Somehow she wasn't surprised to find him there. Though she'd never before slept through the night next to a living soul, it seemed natural to wake up beside Thomas, the curves of their bodies matching.

She blinked the sleep from her eyes and studied him in the morning sunlight. In sleep he looked younger, more like the young man who had sung love ballads around her fireplace than the battle-seasoned knight who had imperiously asked the king for her hand.

There was a stubble of whiskers along the firm line of his jaw. His hair was disheveled, with one thick lock fallen across his forehead. Before she could stop them, her fingers reached up to push it gently back from his face.

Her touch made him stir, but he didn't awaken. She lifted herself on one elbow to study him better. The covers had slipped down from his shoulders to reveal a bare, sculpted chest. The sight set a pulse beating at the side of her neck. All at once she wished, fiercely, that she were truly the servant girl, Rose, who could choose her loves with care-free abandon, heedless of considerations of rank and fortune. She wished it was some other girl who had had to listen to her father's endless ramblings about poor men hunting for riches or rich men hunting for power.

Don't people sometimes just fall in love, Father? She looked up at the wooden beams of the ceiling, sending the silent query up to the heavens. Weren't you simply in love, you and my mother?

Thomas was stirring. His eyes were closed but he reached for her and drew her against his chest. She allowed herself to be pulled against him. His warmth and the strength of his arms around her felt right and comforting and sensual. Banishing all reason, she let herself be enveloped.

He opened his eyes, obviously surprised to find her pliant and willing in his arms. She smiled at him and he drew in a quick breath.

"Alyce?" he asked, sleep still clogging his throat.

"Nay," she whispered. "'Tis Rose. I've come to waken you before the morning sun can rise and catch us at our games."

He turned her slightly so that she rested against one of his arms. "Naughty Rose," he murmured. "What if your mistress catches us?"

"She might have me flogged."

"Aye, she's a hard one." He began to drop light kisses along the edge of her bottom lip.

Alyce shook her head. "Nay, she's not as hard as you think."

Thomas grinned. "I know she's not," he said very softly. He continued the kisses across her upper lip, then moved to her cheeks, her forehead. He kissed her eyes shut, then continued along her temple until Alyce felt as if she were floating in a veritable sea of kisses.

"I did this badly last night, Alyce," Thomas began, his voice serious. "The first thing I should have said is that I—"

But Alyce didn't want words. She lifted herself up to whisper in his ear, "Shh. It's not Alyce, but

Rose—the saucy serving wench who wants nothing more than to spend the morning in lovemaking.''

Thomas was only too happy to oblige. He rolled her over so that she was lying on top of him, their stomachs pressed together. ''I like my wenches saucy,'' he said with a grin. The hardening of his lower body against hers reinforced the words.

She gave a merry laugh and, with her elbows planted on his chest, put a hand along each cheek to feel the scrape of his whiskers against her fingers. ''And I like my men bold,'' she said, her blue eyes flaring.

''Oh, do you now?'' he asked softly. His voice had roughened, and his eyes had grown narrow. In an instant, he flipped her over so that he was on top with her pinned underneath. ''Then bold I'll be,'' he said, before plundering her mouth with his.

It robbed her of breath and of reason. With tongue and lips he stoked a fire of longing that soon had her writhing beneath him, wanting more.

He threw back the covers with sudden impatience, and together they rid themselves of the few clothes they'd worn to sleep, eager to feel the merging of their bare skin. His was almost hot to the touch, still warm from the cocoon of blankets. Hers was cool, but heated instantly everywhere they touched.

He pulled his mouth away and found a breast, then urged it to life with the tip of his tongue. ''I never knew a rose could taste so sweet,'' he murmured as he turned his attentions to the other breast, making the tugging more insistent.

She gave a moan of pleasure at the back of her throat. The waves of feeling had already begun. Sensing her sudden need, he pulled away just long enough to join their bodies. She cried his name, and he held her tightly as completion rocked her.

For several more moments he stayed quiet inside her while he again kissed her neck and her mouth and her breasts. It wasn't long before the feeling began to build anew. This time he moved with her, swiftly, taking her up and up until the intensity burst on them both simultaneously.

For a moment she lay utterly still, while his head came down to lie heavy on her chest. Then she began to laugh. She felt free and incredibly happy, as if every care in the world had been lifted from her. She could feel his answering smile against her breast.

After several moments, he raised his head. ''Was that bold enough for you, milady?'' he asked.

''It was perfect,'' she said with feeling. She smiled up into his eyes. ''Aye, it was perfect.''

''You're the perfect one, sweetheart. And I'm the luckiest man in England to have you belong to me.''

She belonged to no one, came the immediate rebuttal, but she didn't speak the words. She was too happy to argue. For the moment, she just wanted to lie with Thomas and enjoy the kind of simple pleasure that can be achieved between a man and a woman in love.

"I'm glad you came back," she said.

"I came back last night, but you were sleeping so soundly I didn't want to wake you."

"It had been a hard day," she observed with just a trace of irony.

He gathered her in his arms and kissed her gently. "My poor darling. I want to keep you from ever having hard days. That's precisely why I wanted to be your husband—to make you happy and protect you from anything bad."

She didn't want to talk about marriage. "You made me happy this morning," she said, sticking with the safer topic.

"Not as happy as you made me, sweetheart. After last night, I was afraid you'd never let me near you again. What changed your mind?"

She couldn't answer. She couldn't tell him that she had lain awake examining his face in the morning light, and had realized that she was in love with him. "I believe I'm less ill-tempered in the morning hours," she said instead.

He gave a hearty laugh. "I'll remember that. Though now that I'm learning some of your secrets, I might be able to convince you to abandon your ill temper at other hours of the day." He put his hand playfully over one of her bare breasts. "And night," he added with a wicked grin.

She smiled back. "I believe you might at that."

"In fact, shall we test how milady's temper fares at—" he glanced out the guardhouse window at the height of the sun "—*mid*morning?"

She giggled and allowed him to pull her back into his arms. "I have a feeling *midmorning* is also an auspicious time of day," she answered.

Then his mouth closed hers and neither of them talked for a very long time.

"I see my brief sermon last night took effect," Kenton said as he joined his friend in the stables, where Thomas was helping a lad saddle two horses. "I just saw the lady Alyce practically dancing through the hall, whistling one of those love ballads she professes to despise. And you have the appearance of the cook's boy who's managed to secret away an entire apple pastry all for himself."

Thomas grinned. "I've eaten nothing all day," he said.

Kenton shook his head. "That's not wise, my friend. A man in your circumstances needs sustenance." He pulled a crust of bread from his pocket. "Here, eat this before you swoon from hunger."

Thomas waved away his friend's offering. "A man in love doesn't need food," he said.

Kenton groaned. "Ah, Thomas, you've been hit

bad. I take it you've managed to convince the lady that you *do* love her, after all. You've told her so?''

Thomas finished tightening the cinch on his saddle and looked over to see that Alyce's horse was ready. ''I didn't need to tell her. The convincing was done in other ways.''

Kenton shook his head. ''Aye, those ways are good, too. But don't forget about the telling, Thomas. It's as important as the other.''

Thomas grinned at his friend. ''If she were yours, how much time would you waste in talking?''

''As much time as it takes to be sure there are no more misunderstandings between us.''

''Those days are over, Kenton. Alyce and I are in love, and nothing is ever going to come between us again.''

Kenton swatted his friend on the back. ''I suppose that means you're not inviting me to ride along with the two of you this afternoon?''

''Aye, Kent, that's exactly what it means,'' Thomas answered dryly. Then he gathered the reins of both mounts and headed out of the stable.

They'd left behind the crowded streets of Nottingham town and ridden out into the countryside, enjoying the mild air of early spring. Alyce had brought along a basket of food, since they had missed the early meal of the day and were too hungry to wait until evening.

They rode easily, without hurry and without direction, happy to have the strife that had surrounded the betrothal behind them. They could
very well be a servant girl and her swain going out
to picnic on a beautiful day, Alyce thought happily.

They followed alongside a winding stream that
led them up into some gentle hills, taking them out
of sight of the castle and the town.

"It's like we've found our own private world,
Thomas," Alyce said. She was still giddy from the
morning lovemaking and had the craziest impulse
to shout.

"We have, sweetheart, a world of you and me."

"It's a beautiful day," she said, feeling as if
happiness was bubbling out of her.

Thomas pulled his horse to a stop. "Aye. But is
there to be food in this world of ours? For, in truth,
I've worked a hard day's labor already today with
no nourishment."

Alyce wrinkled her nose at him. "Fie on you,
sir, to call it work."

He dismounted and came to lift her off her
horse. "I'm teasing, love. 'Twas the most enjoy-
able morning's labor I've had in a long time."

She slid into his arms, but held him off when he
tried to kiss her. "In a long time?" she asked.

He grinned. "Or ever. Aye, I meant to say
ever."

She laughed and rocked up on her toes to give
him the desired kiss. He held her there a moment,

making it more lingering than either had intended, and they were each a little breathless when they ended the embrace.

"Food," Alyce reminded him.

He looked regretful, but finally said, "Aye, food." Then he amended with a grin, "Food *first*."

She smiled at him over her shoulder as she unfastened the basket from her mount's saddle. Then, while he led the horses down to the stream for some water, she sat on the grassy bank and pulled out two meat pasties wrapped in cloth, and a jug of wine.

Though the kiss had distracted them for a moment, once they started eating they both discovered that they were famished. They finished the juicy pies down to the last crumb and drank much of the wine. When they'd finished, Thomas lay back on the bank with a contented groan. "All the angels of heaven could not offer a more perfect day than this," he said.

She reached for his hand. "I never thought I'd be so happy," she agreed.

He tugged at her fingers until she drew close enough so that their legs touched. "Does that mean you've forgiven me for asking the king for your hand?" he asked.

She didn't answer for a long moment. "I wish you'd asked me instead."

"What would you have said?"

She laughed. "I'm not sure."

"You see?" he said. "I was right to do it my way."

She wasn't going to agree with him, but she didn't want to argue. "So the prophecy came true," she murmured.

Thomas looked blank. "Prophecy?"

"Aye. When I went back to the castle to change my clothes for our ride, Lettie reminded me that old Maeve's prophecy has come true. You remember—that night she said I'd be forced into a betrothal to the king's choice."

Thomas looked unimpressed. "She also said there'd be wolves on the moon or some such nonsense, sweetheart. It's of no account."

"No, the wolves were howling the night she got the vision. The moon was..." She saw that he wasn't interested in the topic. "Anyway, I did have to marry the king's choice. We just didn't know that it would be you."

"But you're now glad that it was."

"Aye."

He seized her hand and planted a kiss in the middle of her palm. Then, his eyes mischievous, he held the palm out and peered intently as if he were reading it. "Ah, milady, I see wonderful things in your future."

She laughed. "What things do you see, oh prophet?"

He turned her hand first one way and then another. "I see you very happy with a wonderful husband."

"Wonderful, is he?"

"Aye, and handsome, too. Brave."

"Modest, as well."

He waggled the hand a little, peered intently, and then said, "Eh, maybe not so modest as some."

She bent down alongside him to stare at her hand. "You see all that in there?"

"Aye," he said. "And children. You'll have a dozen."

"At least," she agreed dryly.

He looked at her palm again. "Aye, at least."

With a giggle, she pulled her hand out of his grasp. "I think you should stick to soldiering and leave the fortune-telling to the gypsies."

"I don't need to be a fortune-teller to see a happy future for us, sweetheart," he told her, his expression serious.

Her voice grew soft. "I hope you're right."

"And you have forgiven me?" he asked again.

She had—almost. "Satisfy my curiosity first. What did you tell the king when you two were alone? Why did he suddenly decide to grant your request about the marriage?"

When Thomas took a long time to answer, she looked down at him and was surprised to see that he appeared to be hiding something. "Thomas?" she asked again.

"'Twas merely a man-to-man conversation," he said with studied nonchalance. "I convinced him that you needed me to protect you."

A wave of cold ran through her. She'd asked the question casually, but now it seemed to take on a significance she hadn't expected. Because for some unknown reason, Thomas was lying to her.

Chapter Fourteen

She knew it as surely as she knew her own name. Whatever it was Thomas had discussed with the king, he didn't want her to know about it. Suddenly the meat pasty felt thick and greasy in her stomach.

"You spoke of nothing else?" she asked.

"Nay. It didn't take much to convince him. The king owed me a favor, and how could he better repay it than by giving me the most beautiful woman in all his kingdom?"

The pretty words danced in her head, but didn't make her happy as they would have a few moments earlier. All the suspicions that her father had planted came back to her. Thomas didn't want her to know what he had told the king. The king owed him a favor. Did the king give her to Thomas as wife because she was beautiful or because the poor knight he sought to reward was looking for a woman of property who could make him rich?

Thomas seemed to realize that the direction of the conversation was causing her distress. "We won't talk about the betrothal anymore, sweetheart. It's done. Let's forget about it and go back to being Thomas and Rose, two simple folk enjoying the pleasures of a beautiful spring day."

She mustered a wan smile. "I wish it were true," she said.

Thomas sat up and pulled her into his arms. "We'll make it true, sweetling. Here, have a drink of wine."

They'd brought no tumblers. He tipped the jug while she drank a big, sweet gulp. Then he helped himself before he stuffed the cork back in the top. Without loosening his hold on her, he leaned over to set the jug a safe distance away in the grass. Then he began to kiss her, gently.

"Two simple folk," he murmured, deepening the kiss.

She didn't resist, but it took several moments before her body once again overruled her head and began to respond to his caresses. Once it did, however, she forgot all about his evasive comments and everything else as all her attention centered on the feel of his mouth and hands on her body.

Soon they both wanted more, but Alyce murmured, "'Tis broad daylight." They looked around, laughing and a little self-conscious, to be sure they were not visible from the road.

"The rabbits and birds will not be offended by

our love play, sweetheart,'' Thomas assured her.
Then, keeping covered by as much clothing as they
could for modesty, they once again came together
in a delicious union.

It was only afterward, as Thomas lay dozing
next to her in the soft grass, that the doubts began
anew. Long ago back at Sherborne, Thomas had
said that he loved her. Their lovemaking certainly
made that appear to be true. But was that truly why
he had married her? Or was he just like all the men
her father had warned her against? Was Thomas
using her to get his hands on Sherborne?

She gave a sigh and sat up to retrieve her
clothes.

'''Tis obvious that the man's in love with ye,
Allie. He doesn't take his eyes off ye, and when
one of the other knights gives ye more than a passing glance, Sir Thomas glowers at the poor man
until he turns in the other direction.''

Lettie was helping Alyce bathe in a tiny tin tub
before she and Thomas were to join the king for
dinner in the great hall. As she had her entire life,
Alyce found herself pouring out her doubts to her
faithful nurse, who was giving them short shrift.

''He could be jealous and still want my estates,''
Alyce pointed out.

''Aye, and what's wrong with that if he's in love
with ye, too? Contrary to what yer father tried to

tell ye yer whole life, luv, there's no shame in a
man having a measure of ambition.''

"But then how can I be sure that he wants me
as much as he does Sherborne?''

Lettie gave Alyce's back a none-too-gentle
scrub. "Lass, any man with eyes to see with and
a head to think with could not help but want ye
for yerself. But if ye don't know that by now, perhaps 'tis a lesson ye'll never learn. In which case,
ye can just go back to Sherborne and live out yer
life as a shriveled up old lady, just like yer nurse.''

Alyce turned around to smile at the older
woman. "You're not the least bit shriveled, Lettie
dear. And you have many more years before I'll
let you call yourself old. The two of us shall grow
old together.''

Lettie's eyes were sad. "I'd not wish such a life
on ye, Allie. Ye should love and be loved, then
spread yer love to children and grandchildren. But
to do all that, ye have to be willing to have faith
in love itself. Ye could start by putting a little more
trust in the man who's to be yer husband.''

Alyce shivered, her wet skin grown chilly. She
sank deeper into the water, then went back to her
original question. "But why didn't he want to tell
me about his conversation with Richard?''

"I think ye should ask him,'' Lettie said. "Get
it straight.'' She turned aside, avoiding her
charge's direct gaze.

Alyce sat up again, sloshing water out of the tub.

"Lettie? Do you know something you're not telling me?"

The nurse hesitated, then shook her head. "Not really."

Alyce crossed her arms in front of her. "Tell me," she demanded.

"Honestly, Alyce, I don't know anything. Like I told ye, the man's in love with ye."

"But you did hear something?"

With obvious reluctance, the older woman said, "I'll admit that after ye two left for the hall last night, there was some talk among the knights."

Alyce was shivering in earnest now, but she paid no attention. "What kind of talk?"

"They were saying that it was fortunate that Sherborne was in safe hands. I didn't really understand it all that well, lass. 'Twas men's talk."

Her expression told Alyce that Lettie didn't want her to pursue the question any further, but Alyce refused to let up. "Whatever it was they were saying, Lettie, you understood it perfectly. So you might as well tell me."

Lettie sighed and reached for a towel. "They were saying that although Sherborne is small, it would serve as a good strategic point to hold the northwest for Prince John. That's why Baron Dunstan wanted the estate."

It wasn't hard to imagine the rest. Alyce spoke softly. "So now that King Richard is going to the Continent once again, leaving the kingdom vulnerable to John, it's much better for Sherborne to be held by a supporter of Richard.''

Lettie bit her lip. ''There was some such talk,'' she admitted.

''By a faithful supporter of Richard's such as Sir Thomas Brand,'' Alyce added.

Lettie gave a reluctant sigh. ''Aye. But 'tis as I said, Allie, that doesn't mean the man doesn't love ye.''

Alyce remained silent as Lettie helped her rise from the tub and dry herself. When she'd first met Thomas, he'd been risking his life, traveling under a false name raising money for the king's ransom. She knew his loyalty to Richard was fierce. So fierce that he would even be willing to marry if it would further the king's interests. She had no doubt of it.

But was that the only reason he'd wanted to marry her? Lettie said that he was in love with her, and Alyce herself had felt that same thing, at least in their closest moments together.

She thought back to the time she and Thomas had first made love, at Sherborne. For long, wonderful moments, she'd experienced a closeness that she'd never known before with any human being. But abruptly, the closeness had been shattered. By talk of Dunstan and duty. Their disagreement unresolved, Thomas had ridden away, in the service of his lord, King Richard.

She stepped out of the tub and sat on the edge

of her bed while Lettie dried her long hair. "Ye will give it a chance, Allie, won't ye?" Lettie asked finally after a long silence. "'Tis yer chance for happiness, lass."

Alyce thought about the afternoon she and Thomas had just spent on the riverbank. At the end of their lovemaking Thomas had held her for endless moments, crooning a love ballad in her ear. "I love you, Alyce Rose," he'd said, his voice deep with conviction. Surely it was not all a ruse.

"Aye," she told her nurse. "I'll give it a chance."

Philip of Dunstan crumpled the message and threw it across his counting room. The clerk who had brought it to him looked over at it, wondering if he should scurry to retrieve the page for his master or leave it lying in the dust.

"When did this arrive?" Dunstan asked the young man.

"Not an hour ago, milord. The messenger came straight from the prince."

"He's turning into a coward." Dunstan sneered.

The clerk's eyes went wide. After a moment's hesitation, he stuttered, "Aye, mi-milord."

Dunstan rose and pounded both fists on the solid oak table. "I've told him that he needs to act now to get his forces in place. As soon as Richard leaves, we must be ready to move. But the fop lingers at his Easter holidays in London and refuses to listen.''

"Mayhap he's afraid of angering the king," the clerk ventured.

"Aye, and mayhap he doesn't deserve the crown I've been trying to place on his head," Dunstan roared, stalking toward the hapless clerk. The baron's face had gone almost as red as the tunic he wore. "Meanwhile as he dallies, he's costing me a bride.''

The clerk began taking steps backward so as not to be trampled by his enraged master. "Perhaps the message is a mistake, milord. There can be no church marriages during Lent, so—''

"'Tis a betrothal, not a marriage," Dunstan shouted. "Which means that Brand has had first dip into the delectable Lady Sherborne's pot.''

The clerk winced at his master's crudity. He'd backed up as far as he could without leaving the room, and still Dunstan advanced.

"The wench should have been mine," the baron said, towering over his cringing servant.

"Aye, milord.''

"And so she shall be." His voice was suddenly quiet. The red drained from his face as he straightened up with a chilling smile. "And so she shall be," he said again.

The clerk bobbed his head several times in agreement, then, at the baron's wave of dismissal, dashed out of the room with a sigh of relief.

* * *

It wasn't difficult to keep her promise to Lettie. The inclination of her heart made it easy to forget about what Thomas's motive might be for wanting her, and just rejoice in the fact that he *did* want her. In fact, it had become almost an embarrassment, since it seemed that the two of them couldn't go more than a few hours without seeking out each other's company, and once they were together, the urge to steal away for more delicious lovemaking inevitably took over.

"We've created a scandal, Thomas," she told him as they lay in bed on Easter morning, when everyone else in the castle was at the church to witness the opening of the Easter sepulchre and the return of the cross to the altar.

"The court will always find something to gossip about," he said, unconcerned. He was occupying himself with making a braid in her hair. He'd pulled the long tresses to the front, where they reached past her naked breasts. As he wove the strands, his hands occasionally brushed the tips of her nipples.

"They say we do nothing but lie in bed all day making love," she protested.

Thomas stopped his hairdressing for a moment to grin at her. "Aye, and they're sick with envy."

She laughed. "I'm serious. Lettie has scolded me more than once. She says people will think I'm a loose woman."

"Nonsense. You've been with only one man, and you're legally betrothed to him. There's nothing scandalous about it."

"But we seem to…*need* it all the time. Is it normal, do you think?"

Thomas had resumed his weaving, but he laughed. "I'd say that any man betrothed to you who did *not* want it all the time was *not* normal."

Alyce closed her eyes and lay quiet, enjoying the light movements of his hands and her hair against her skin. Her nipples had grown hard and started sending signals to the rest of her body. She tried to tamp down the urges. She and Thomas had already made love twice that morning. Perhaps such excess was normal for a man, but she wasn't sure that it was quite decent in a woman.

She opened her eyes. "Well, this morning, for example, we should be in church. What will people say?"

The braid was completed. "What can we bind it with?" he asked, looking around.

"There's a ribbon over on that chest."

He frowned. "Too far away. I'd have to get out of this warm bed." Instead, he took the end of the braid and began to use it like a little brush, lightly stroking her chin, then her nose. "It's too cold to get up," he repeated.

"But what will people say?" she asked again.

He swept a little path from her chin down to the hollow between her breasts. "Now that Lent's over, we can go ahead with the wedding. Then no one will have a right to say anything.''

The hair tickled, and Alyce felt a chill run down her bare skin all the way to her feet. "You're anxious for the wedding?'' she asked.

She had the feeling that Thomas was paying little attention to the conversation. He'd taken the tuft of hair and was using it to play with her nipples.

"Aye,'' he said absently. "Richard will be leaving soon. It would be best to get it done.''

Best for whom? she wondered. Best for the two of them to start a happy life together? Or best for Thomas Brand, loyal servant to the king? She shivered.

Thomas laughed and dropped the braid to gather her in his arms. "I'm sorry, sweetheart, I didn't mean to tickle you. Now I've given you chills.''

He rolled her over and pulled the covers more closely up around them.

"I didn't mind,'' she said, trying to pull her mind from the topic of marriage.

"No? Then perhaps I'll think up some other ways to torture you.'' He wiggled his eyebrow suggestively.

His teasing made her laugh, and soon she *had* forgotten completely about marriage or any other topic that required reason.

By the time they reluctantly pulled themselves from the bed an hour later, the carefully woven braid was only a memory.

* * *

The week between Easter and Hocktide was a holiday for the villeins of the town and shire. The Nottingham market would be running all week, and various festivities were planned, including games, a mummer's play and a mock joust with tilting at a quintain. On Easter itself, several delegations from the town had brought eggs to the castle to present to the king, and he had thrown open his hall to feed as many of the prominent citizens as could crowd in.

Thomas and Alyce drifted happily from one activity to another, regularly finding time by themselves for more intimate entertainment. He hadn't mentioned again the idea of taking their marriage vows, though with the proscription time of Lent ended, the wedding could be held anytime.

Alyce was grateful not to face the question. But as spring blossomed in the countryside around Nottingham, she found her thoughts returning often to Sherborne. By now the crops of oats, peas, beans and barley should have been planted. She wondered how Fredrick and Alfred were managing in her absence. Had Fredrick gone through with his plan to leave some of the fields lying fallow? she wondered. Were the wheat and rye crops she'd had planted earlier this winter flourishing?

Thomas noticed her distraction as they sat on a hillside watching the end of a mummers' pageant depicting the classic battle of St. George and the dragon.

"Are you tired, sweetheart?" he asked her, then teased, "'tis your own fault for keeping me up half the night."

"We could debate who kept whom awake," she scolded with a smile.

The mummers were dragging away the remnants of the defeated dragon, which looked nowhere near as fierce now that it lay in pieces on the grass. "If you're tired, we could go back to the castle and take an afternoon nap," he suggested.

She gave a little huff. "I suspect your motives, sir," she said.

He grinned. "Wise lady."

Her answering smile had a touch of sadness. She'd been happy these past few days, forgetting all else except the new pleasures she was learning with Thomas. But it was time for her to make some decisions. She had a responsibility to Sherborne and to herself. If Thomas was to be her husband, it was time that she reconciled herself to the idea, time that she, in truth, *stopped* suspecting his motives. And it was time for her to go home.

"When is the king to leave?" she asked him.

He looked surprised at the question. "Soon, I suspect. He's been closeted with his ministers daily, hasn't even been out to enjoy the holiday."

Alyce took a deep breath. "And you want him in attendance at our wedding?"

Thomas went very still. "Aye," he said carefully. "I would like it. It would be an honor." He looked at her, his expression serious. "But it's not essential. I'll do whatever makes you happy."

She looked down the hillside. The grassy clearing that had served as a stage was empty, except for one tattered piece of the dragon's tail that had been inadvertently left behind.

"The spring planting should be nearly finished at Sherborne," she said.

"Aye, and Sherborne's mistress is anxious to see that it's been done." He leaned over and kissed her on the cheek. "Sweetheart, I know that we've neglected our duties these past few days, but I think we've needed this time for ourselves."

She nodded. "But as you say, even the king is choosing duty over merriment this week. We can't forget the rest of the world forever."

He sighed. "Nay. In fact, I've been called to Richard's council this very afternoon. Will you miss me?"

She smiled. "Mayhap I'll take a nap—a *real* nap."

He stood and held his hand out to her. "Then we'll start back to the castle. But why did you ask if I wanted Richard at our wedding?"

She let him pull her up, then brushed the dry grass off the back of her skirt. "Because," she said, her voice determined, "if 'tis to happen, we'd best get it done."

Thomas's face lit up. "I swore I'd not pressure you this time. I don't want to risk being turned away from my bridal bed."

She smiled. "Promise me never to break my heart, and I promise never to turn you away from our bed."

He seized her shoulders and, heedless of the crowds of villagers still milling about in the aftermath of the performance, drew her to him for a long kiss. "I promise, sweetheart. Your heart is safe in my care."

They'd chosen the cloth-of-gold tunic again. It was the only garment Lettie declared fit for a wedding that would be held in the presence of the king.

Lettie had been fussing over her all morning, which had done nothing to calm Alyce's jitters. In spite of Thomas's promise never to break her heart, the doubts she'd been pushing away since Lettie had told her about the importance of Sherborne to both Prince John and the king had wriggled their way to the surface.

She should have sat down with Thomas to discuss the issue, out in the open, but once she had agreed to the wedding, things had moved too fast for any kind of prolonged conversation.

Thomas had spent the afternoon with Richard, and when he had emerged, he'd declared with a triumphant smile that the wedding had been arranged for the following day, with Richard and all his ministers in attendance. Then there had been the dinner, with Kenton and Ranulf vying to see which one could make prettier toasts to the bride-to-be.

Thomas joined in every one, happy and flushed, and by the time they retired to their chamber that evening, he'd been more than a little intoxicated. With a mumbled apology, he'd fallen asleep immediately, without even kissing her good-night.

In the morning, he'd been contrite, but also in a hurry to be off to a final strategy meeting with Richard, since after the wedding he and his new bride would be leaving for Sherborne.

The whole thing had left Alyce bemused, half regretting her decision, but she allowed Lettie to spin her romantic fantasies and wax nostalgic, as befitting the hours before a girl was about to take the vows that would forever alter her life.

"Ah, Allie, yer sainted mother should be here to see ye. She'd be so proud. Yer father, too, of course, but yer mother would have loved to see how beautiful ye've become and what a fine young man ye've found to share yer life with."

Alyce's smile was sad. "Aye, a girl would like to have her mother around on a day like today." She stood up from the stool where she'd been sitting while Lettie finished the last touches on her hair, and enveloped her nurse in a big hug. "But though I can't have my mother, I have the woman who has been a mother to me for as long as I can remember. Lettie, dear, I love you.''

Lettie wiped away tears with the edge of her sleeve. ''And I love ye, Allie, ye little scamp. I want nothing more in this lifetime than to see ye happy.''

''I am happy, Lettie,'' she assured her. ''And if Thomas truly loves me as much as you say he does, then we'll be happy together.''

With a resolute sniff, Lettie made one last adjustment to the circlet of pearls around her head, then stepped back. ''Ye're perfect, lass, and if Thomas Brand doesn't love ye the way ye deserve, then he'll have me to reckon with.''

Alyce grinned. ''And the entire population of Sherborne, as well, I suspect,'' she added. ''I'm a lucky lady to have so many people to support me.''

There was a solid rapping on the door. '''Tis time,'' Lettie said, her eyes filling all over again.

Alyce walked over to the door herself and pulled it open, assuming that Thomas had come for her. To her surprise, it was Ranulf.

''Where's Thomas?'' she asked.

His expression was serious. ''He's with the king. They're meeting with the ministers.''

''Shouldn't they be going to the church by now?'' Lettie asked with a frown.

Ranulf shook his head. His blue eyes, so like his brother's, were full of concern. ''Thomas sent me to fetch you, Lady Alyce. I'm sorry, but I don't think there's going to be a wedding today.''

Chapter Fifteen

She'd waited in the antechamber for over an hour, alternately pacing the floor and sitting nervously in the window seat next to Ranulf, who was as much in the dark as she about what was transpiring behind the closed doors of the king's receiving room.

"All I know is that Thomas sent Kenton to find me, with instructions to go to you and tell you that the wedding would be delayed," Ranulf had told her with a smile of apology.

"And now Kenton is with them inside?"

"Aye."

"What could they be talking about?"

Ranulf shrugged. "Something too important for women or knights who've not yet earned their spurs," he said.

She sensed that he was feeling the same resentment as she for being left out.

"Something important enough to postpone a

wedding that your brother professed to want more than anything,'' she added.

Ranulf gave her a sympathetic glance. ''He did want it, milady. He *does* want it. He's crazy in love with you.''

She shrugged. ''Everyone seems to tell me that but your brother himself.'' Once again she rose to her feet to pace the length of the chamber.

By the time the meeting ended, Alyce had gone from hurt to angry.

Thomas went to her immediately. ''Forgive me, sweetheart,'' he said, his voice distracted. ''The timing on this was unfortunate.''

''Aye,'' she agreed.

He didn't appear to notice the flare of fire in her eyes. ''We've been discussing tactics. I shouldn't reveal much to you, since it's safer for you not to know, but I do need to tell you one thing.''

She could almost feel the steam rising from her hot cheeks. ''And what might that be?'' she asked.

''Philip of Dunstan has taken over Sherborne Castle.''

She gasped and took a step backward. She'd thought her problems with Dunstan were over now that she'd been betrothed to Thomas, but it seemed as if the man was going to bedevil her the rest of her life.

Thomas took hold of her elbow to support her. ''I'm sorry. It's my fault for not posting men there immediately after our betrothal. I didn't expect him to make such a move.''

"Nor did I," she agreed. "But what about my people? There has been no violence? Is everyone all right?''

He nodded. "We had no reports of anyone putting up resistance. I assume that with you not there…" His voice trailed off.

"It was easy for the baron's men to walk in and take over," she finished.

"Aye." He looked away, his face glum.

"I'm going home," she said. "I'll start immediately.''

He snapped his head back to look at her. "You most assuredly will not," he said. "The last thing we need is for Dunstan to seize you as a hostage.''

"When he came before, he let me go as soon as he heard about King Richard's return. I don't think he'd dare hurt me.''

"I'm not willing to take the risk. Last time, he hadn't had time to consult with Prince John. This time he has, and evidently it's part of the prince's strategy to consolidate his hold over England.''

"Which makes a little place like Sherborne important?" she asked, already knowing the answer to her question.

"Aye. As soon as Richard leaves the country this time, we believe John will have everything in place to seize the crown for himself.''

Alyce's head was pounding. She put her hands

to her temples. "I don't care about John or Richard. I just want Sherborne to be left in peace."

Thomas bent to give her a quick kiss. "And so it shall, sweetheart. I'm going to see to it. In the meantime, don't you worry about it."

"Don't worry about it?" She shook her head in disbelief.

He paused. "Well, try not to. I'll send word back as soon as I can."

"You won't have to send word anywhere, because if you're riding to Sherborne, I'm riding with you."

Ranulf had politely remained in his window seat to allow them to talk privately, but when he saw the expression on his brother's face, he stood and walked over to them. "What's going on, Thomas?" he asked.

"It's Dunstan again. He's seized Sherborne Castle, and my stubborn bride is determined that she's going to charge right up there."

"It's her castle," Ranulf said mildly.

Alyce shot him a smile.

"Aye, it's her castle, but it could be her life if Dunstan gets hold of her. She's staying safely here at Nottingham until we take care of this."

"Nay, I'm not," Alyce said firmly.

Ranulf looked from one implacable face to the other, then asked brightly, "So…are we still planning a wedding for this afternoon?"

* * *

There had been no wedding. Alyce had ridden with Thomas and his men to Sherborne.

King Richard himself had decided it. "She's the lady of Sherborne, Thomas," he'd said. "She has an interest in seeing it safely back in her keeping."

Her victory came at the cost of Thomas's anger. He'd scarcely spoken to her on the road, and she knew that if she gave him the least cause, he'd send her straight back to Nottingham, bound hand and foot, if necessary. For the most part, she stayed away from him, riding with Ranulf, who Thomas had grudgingly let join the party at the last minute.

"My brother just wants to keep you safe, Alyce," the young knight told her as they moved along toward the back of the procession, which included all the "Havilland" knights, plus a number of King Richard's soldiers.

"I know, but I have the right to make the decision for myself. He should understand that."

Ranulf nodded sympathetically. "He's used to telling people what to do, I'm afraid. And he's always been stubborn."

"Pigheaded, I'd call it," she grumbled.

"Thomas may have finally met his match, however," he said with a grin.

She answered his smile briefly with one of her own, but it was short-lived. She was too worried about what she would find when they reached Sherborne to stay lighthearted for long.

After a day and a half of hard riding, they

reached the outskirts of Sherborne. Thomas had sent men ahead to find them a secluded campsite where they could rest and reconnoiter until they found out the status inside the castle.

He had little to say to Alyce after their arrival, other than to tell her that a tent had been set up for her at one edge of the camp if she was tired. But she was far too worried to sleep, and when Thomas called a meeting on a small hill above the campsite that afternoon, she insisted on attending.

"How can you be certain what's going on inside?" she demanded. She was sitting with Kenton and some of Richard's knights at the far end of the circle from Thomas. He had ignored her until her question made that no longer possible.

"Fantierre has sent word of conditions inside the castle," he said tersely.

Alyce was surprised. "He is still with Dunstan? I thought he would rejoin Richard as soon as the King came back to England."

Thomas shook his head. "It was decided that Dunstan would continue to bear watching, especially since Richard is to leave again so soon."

"Did he say who the hostages are?" she asked, willing herself to keep her voice steady, though her insides were trembling. The word from inside Sherborne was that the Dunstan forces were in peaceful control of the castle, a peace that was guaranteed by the holding of prisoners. Dunstan had threatened that any incidence of resistance against his men would mean that one of the prisoners would be executed.

Thomas shook his head. "He has several. Two of them are children. One is your chamberlain."

Alyce closed her eyes. Poor old Alfred. He was too frail to stand up to any rough treatment.

"Dunstan's men are good fighters," Kenton said.

Martin the Reaper sat on the other side of him. He looked up with a grim smile. "Not as good as we are," he said. "I say we go in and take them."

Thomas shook his head. "A pitched battle would cost Sherborne lives as well as some of our own."

Kenton looked angry. "That's what Prince John and Dunstan are counting on. England's at peace. They don't think we want to start another bloody civil war, to go back to the days when Saxons and Normans vied for how many villages they could pillage."

"Still, the king sent us to scope out the problem, not to fight a battle," Thomas said calmly. "In the meantime, three other castles have been taken over by John's supporters."

"They're waiting for Richard to cross the Channel again, and then they'll make their move," Martin said, and several of the other men around the circle nodded in agreement.

Alyce was feeling increasingly frustrated by the conversation. She didn't care about John or Richard. All she knew was that *her* people were in jeopardy. And no one seemed to know what to do about it.

"I'll go speak to Dunstan myself," she said loudly.

Every male head in the circle turned to look at her. Some wore smiles, but most looked simply annoyed.

Thomas didn't bother to comment on her offer. "The king has sent men to the other castles in question. What we need is an overall strategy. My advice would be for him to meet with Prince John directly. They are brothers, after all."

"But they've been enemies since childhood," Kenton pointed out.

Thomas stood. "I need to report what we've found to the king. If we're to make some kind of agreement with John, Richard is the only one who can do it." He looked around the circle, his gaze skirting over Alyce. "Kenton, I'm going to leave you in charge here. You're not to make a move. Just sit tight and wait for me to work things out with Richard."

Kenton nodded, while Alyce looked on in amazement.

"You're leaving?" she asked in disbelief.

"I'll speak with you in private, Alyce," he told her, obviously not wanting their discussion to be shared by the circle of men.

The knights took their cue. Quickly they got up

and started down the hill toward the makeshift camp. In moments, Thomas and Alyce were left alone.

"How can you speak of leaving when this very minute Dunstan may be torturing or killing my people?" she asked him.

His face was hard. He looked nothing at all like the tender, teasing man she had spent so many hours making love to over the past few days. "We have no choice. To go in with a mounted force would surely cause Dunstan to react against your people. This is a time for diplomacy, and for that I need to go back to Nottingham."

"Why can't we try your diplomacy directly with Dunstan? You and I could go speak with him."

"All we would be doing is giving him two more hostages to hold against Richard, *valuable* hostages this time."

"*My people* are valuable," she said, raising her voice.

He looked down at the campsite and motioned for her to be quiet. "Of course they are, sweetheart. But walking into Dunstan's trap is not going to help them any."

His endearment made her tone softer, but she was still indignant. "We can't just sit here."

"I'd prefer you didn't," he said. "I'd like to take you back with me to Nottingham."

She gave a stubborn shake of her head. "I'm not going anywhere."

His nod was resigned. "I suspected as much. But you're not to do anything foolish. I'm going to tell Kenton to watch out for your welfare."

"And you're really leaving?" she asked. Suddenly, she realized that, in spite of her anger, his presence gave her a feeling of hope. It made her feel braver and stronger.

He took hold of her shoulders. "The only way this is going to be resolved is by Richard and John working things out between themselves. Someone has to tell that to the king."

"You could send Kenton," she said, her voice grown small.

"Nay. I'm in charge. It's up to me to see this thing through. Besides—" he gave her a wan smile "—Sherborne is my responsibility now. We were interrupted, but if you remember, the lady of Sherborne is about to become my wife."

Was all of this concern because he wanted to protect *his* property? she wondered. Her chin went up. "Go then, if you must," she said stiffly.

"You'll not come back with me?" he asked again.

"Nay."

He stood a long moment looking into her eyes. His own were inscrutable. Finally, he said, "Do not be tempted to try any of your harebrained adventures, Alyce Rose, or I swear I'll give you the well-deserved spanking that you never got from your softhearted nurse all those years."

She wrinkled her nose at him. "I think little of bullies who threaten those weaker than themselves," she said. "But I learned my lesson at Dunstan Castle. I promise not to endanger any of your men again."

He nodded, satisfied. Then he gave her a quick, hard kiss and strode away toward the horses.

They'd been waiting for an agonizingly long five days and were running low on food. Kenton had taken Harry the Stout and Martin to a nearby town for supplies. Ranulf stayed behind to serve as Alyce's unofficial bodyguard, though there was no need for protection among the men in the camp.

In spite of her worry over what was going on at Sherborne, she never failed to smile and offer a kind word to the men who brought her food or built up the fires or performed any of the other little services to make her more comfortable. Passing among them, gracious and beautiful with her long blond hair, she had come to be looked at by the soldiers of the camp as something like a guardian angel.

Though she had no need of a guard, she was glad that Ranulf had stayed. She enjoyed the young knight's company. In some ways it was like having Thomas around. The resemblance was strong, and he had much of his big brother's charm. But with Ranulf there was none of the tension she felt with

Thomas. She didn't have to worry about considerations of marriage and motives.

"Admit it, Alyce," Ranulf was saying as the two sat together under a tree, some distance from the rest of the camp. "You are as much in love with my brother as he is with you."

She smiled sadly. "If Thomas is so much in love with me, why isn't he here?"

"Because he's busy working to find a way to get Dunstan out of Sherborne without bloodshed."

"Aye," she said without much conviction.

Ranulf spoke more vehemently. "He *is,* Alyce. He's doing this for you—for love of you."

"And love of Richard and, no doubt, love of himself," she added.

Ranulf leaned back against the tree with a little cluck of disgust. "I don't believe you're as cynical as you try to pretend. I think you're in love with him, and you know that he loves you."

She didn't want to argue the issue. The worry and the discomfort of sleeping on the hard ground had left her tired and irritable. The happy days she and Thomas had spent together in Nottingham Castle seemed a lifetime away.

"You're a loyal brother," she told Ranulf, closing the discussion.

Ranulf's gaze was directed to the far side of the campsite, where a horseman had appeared. "We have a visitor," he said, standing.

Alyce recognized the man at once. "'Tis the

Frenchman, Fantierre,'' she said, jumping up.
''He's come from Sherborne.''

They both took off at a run and had crossed the
camp by the time Fantierre dismounted from his
horse.

''Lady Sherborne,'' he greeted her, obviously
surprised at her presence.

Ranulf stepped forward and offered his hand.
''I'm Thomas's brother,'' he told the man.

Fantierre shook his hand and nodded. ''I can see
the resemblance,'' he said, but obviously was not
interested in spending more time on socializing.
''Thomas has gone back to Nottingham?''

Ranulf nodded.

''Where's Kenton?'' Fantierre asked tersely.

''On a supply foray with a couple of our men,''
Ranulf told him.

Fantierre shook his head. ''I can't wait. I need
to be back at the castle before I'm missed.''

''What's happening there?'' Alyce asked. ''Can
you tell us? Is Alfred all right—the old chamberlain?''

Fantierre gave her a quick smile of reassurance.
''No one has been hurt, at least not yet.''

''Not yet?'' she asked, her hands clasped nervously.

''There's been a little problem with the young
man. I believe he's the chamberlain's grandson.''

''Fredrick?''

''*Oui*, Fred-e-rick. He tried to get them to release his grandfather, and now they're holding him. Dunstan says he intends to hang him as an example to the others.''

"Hang him?" Ranulf asked.

Alyce clutched at her throat.

"Aye," Fantierre confirmed grimly. "I was hoping to find Thomas here."

"We haven't heard from him," Ranulf said. "He went back to Nottingham to try to convince King Richard to meet with Prince John. If the two brothers can reach some kind of a settlement, there will be no reason for Dunstan to hold Sherborne. He thinks it would be the best solution for everyone.''

Fantierre shrugged. "He's probably right. I just hope the agreement comes in time for your Frede-rick," he said to Alyce. "He's a brave young man."

Alyce looked at Ranulf. "We have to do something."

Ranulf's usually sunny face was worried. "Milady...Alyce, I'm sorry, but we can't do anything but wait. Thomas left strict orders."

"We can't just sit here while Fredrick's life is in danger." She turned to Fantierre, but the Frenchman supported Ranulf.

"Any movement by these troops would no doubt put a lot of other people's lives in danger, milady. You'd do best to listen to young Brand here."

Alyce looked from one man to the other, unable to believe that they would offer no solution when Fredrick's life was hanging in the balance. "You intend to do nothing?" she asked again.

Ranulf looked down at the ground, and Fantierre gave another of his Gallic shrugs.

"Then excuse me, gentleman," she said, brushing past them and heading toward the nearby grove where the horses had been hobbled. "I need to be going."

Fantierre and Ranulf watched in disbelief as she marched over to the horses and began telling the guard who was caring for them to saddle her mount.

"Where does she think she's going?" Fantierre asked.

Ranulf gave a deep sigh. "I don't know, but my hunch would be Sherborne Castle."

"By herself?"

Ranulf shook his head and started after Alyce. "Nay," he said over his shoulder. "With me."

Fantierre followed him, leading his mount. "You both are crazy," he said to Ranulf's back.

By the time the two men reached Alyce, she'd helped the guard ready her horse and was asking him to give her a boost up into the saddle.

"What do you think you're doing, milady?" Ranulf asked, his voice resigned.

"I'm going to pay a visit on Philip of Dunstan," she said. "I'm going to make sure he doesn't mistreat any more of my people."

Chapter Sixteen

Between the two of them, Ranulf and Fantierre had managed to convince her that riding straight into Sherborne Castle without any forethought would be of little help to Fredrick. Most likely Dunstan would seize Alyce as a hostage as well, and still hang her young servant.

"Then help me figure out some kind of plan to help him," she begged the two men.

"Let's at least wait until Kenton comes back," Ranulf urged.

"I need to get back to the castle myself," Fantierre reminded him. "If you want my help with a plan, we need to figure it out now."

Though she hadn't confessed it to anyone, Alyce had been formulating an idea for the past two days. "When your brother's men first came to Sherborne," she told Ranulf, "I poisoned them."

"You what?" he asked, astonished.

"Well, I sickened them. I thought they'd come from Dunstan, so I had my cooks feed them meat that had gone bad."

Fantierre laughed. "*Ma chère,* it's no wonder Thomas fell in love with you."

Ranulf looked at them both as if they'd taken leave of their senses. "You might have killed someone," he said to Alyce.

She gave a contrite nod. "But I didn't. They are all hale and well, as you can see." She gestured toward the camp, where the men milled about or lay on their bedrolls, bored, waiting for some action.

"What does this have to do with our present situation?" Ranulf asked. "Don't tell me you want to feed bad meat to Dunstan's men."

Alyce shook her head. "Not meat, no." She paused and looked from one man to the other, her eyes sparking with excitement. "I want to drug them."

Fantierre grew serious. "I hate to say this, *chèrie,* but you're not going to find Dunstan as easy to trick as Thomas was. The baron is on his guard, and if anything should go wrong..." He gave his customary shrug and ran his finger across his neck to simulate the slitting of a throat.

"Would he dare do such a thing when she's under the protection of the king?" Ranulf asked.

Fantierre nodded. "Let me put it this way. The beautiful lady Alyce would disappear, never to be seen again. And no one would be able to hold Dunstan accountable for the crime.''

''I think we'd better wait for Thomas,'' Ranulf said fervently.

Fantierre made a move to get on his horse. ''*Oui,* it's best. I need to get back.''

''No, wait,'' Alyce begged, putting her hand on the Frenchman's sleeve. ''I'm not being reckless. I've thought this out and it could work.''

Fantierre gave her an admiring smile. ''Most definitely I see why my friend Thomas is in love with you, *ma belle.*''

She paid little heed to the compliment. ''There's a woman in Sherborne village—old Maeve, they call her.''

''Ah *oui,* I've heard them speak of her. She's a witch, they say.''

''I don't know if she's witch or not, but she knows herbs, and she has powerful medicines that can make men sleep for *hours.*'' Alyce stopped to see if Ranulf and Fantierre seemed to be following her words. She had the feeling that if she'd been trying to explain her plan to Thomas and Kenton, by now they'd have stopped listening and walked away. But both Ranulf and Fantierre were still paying attention.

''And you think you can feed this medicine to Dunstan's soldiers?'' Fantierre asked.

She nodded. ''And when they're sleeping, Richard's forces can come in and take over without anyone getting hurt."

Fantierre shook his head in amazement. "A woman's view of warfare," he said. He sounded guardedly excited. "But it's so crazy that it just might have some possibilities."

Ranulf looked doubtful. "How would you get the drug to Dunstan's men?"

"Maeve will tell me. Most likely in the ale. No one can go long without a drink. We'll put it in just before the evening meal. By midnight the entire castle will be sleeping like babes."

"Would we get the drug to Fantierre and let him doctor the ale?" Ranulf asked.

Alyce shook her head. "No. We'd need the co-operation of my people. I'll have to go to the castle myself."

"I can't let you do that, milady," Ranulf said at once. "Thomas would tear my head off."

Alyce brushed past him and started to mount her horse. "Then tell him I left you no choice, Ranulf."

The young knight looked miserable. "I beg you, Lady Alyce, wait until we hear something from Thomas."

She shook her head. "By then Fredrick could be dead. Don't worry, Ranulf. I'll explain things to Thomas after the deed is done."

"I doubt he'll wait for an explanation before he throttles me," he said glumly.

Alyce smiled down at him from her horse. "Tell him I drugged you as well," she suggested.

Fantierre had made up his mind. Quickly he pulled himself into the saddle. "I'll ride back with you," he said. "I'll tell them I found you wandering about and took you prisoner. We'll try to keep you away from Dunstan until your people have time to use the herbs at tonight's meal."

"Thank you, Fantierre. We'll stop at old Maeve's on the way to the castle." Alyce turned to Ranulf. "Kenton should be back soon. Can you and he get the men together to come into the castle tonight?"

"What if the herbs don't work?"

Alyce's face was set. "They've got to work. Come an hour after midnight. I'll open the front gates."

Obviously unhappy, Ranulf nodded, then stepped back as the two riders spurred their horses and rode off.

Fortunately, it appeared to be a "good" day. Old Maeve's dark eyes were bright with intelligence, and she wasted little time mixing a pouch of medicine from the contents of the vials and odd little boxes that filled the shelves in her tiny cottage.

"They will sleep, no doubt of it," Maeve said firmly. "Even the biggest and strongest knight will sleep like a babe."

"And just one mug of ale is enough?" Alyce asked.

"Half a mug is enough," Maeve assured her.

Alyce looked at Fantierre, who nodded approval. "You'll have to warn your own people to go thirsty this night," he said.

"Aye." She looked at Maeve. "Can this hurt anyone, Maeve?"

The old woman nodded and carefully lowered herself into a chair next to her small fireplace. "Too much can kill a man."

"Kill him?"

"Aye. It's a powerful drug."

Once again, Alyce turned to Fantierre, who shrugged. "Do we have any other choice?" he asked.

Alyce shook her head. "I don't want to harm anyone. I just want my castle back and my people safe."

"Two will die," Maeve said. Her voice had suddenly lowered, and Alyce recognized the look that came into the old woman's eyes when she was having one of her visions. Her words made Alyce freeze.

"Two will die?" she asked. "Two of Dunstan's soldiers?"

Old Maeve's eyes closed and she began to rock. "Two will die before the setting of the blood moon," she said.

Alyce looked helplessly at Fantierre. "She appears to have gone out of her head," he said.

"It happens when her visions come on her," Alyce explained. "What do you think we should do?"

"Personally, I don't think it would be a great tragedy to lose one or two of Dunstan's men," Fantierre said. "And if we kill off Dunstan himself, we will be doing the world a favor."

Alyce was not satisfied. She knelt in front of the old woman and grasped both her hands. "We don't want to kill anyone, Maeve. Tell us how we can use the medicine safely."

But Maeve didn't appear to hear. A tiny stream of spittle made its way out of the corner of her mouth as she rocked back and forth, and once again she began mumbling in her own strange language.

Alyce stood. "There's nothing we can do for her now. She has to work through these spells naturally."

Fantierre picked up the pouch of powder and hefted it in his hand. "So we go ahead with the plan?"

"I don't like it," Alyce said, "but as you say, what other choice do we have?"

"The die is cast, milady," Fantierre said. "Now we play out the rest of the game." He looked at old Maeve. "Do we leave her like this?"

"Aye. There's nothing more we can do for her."

With the old woman still muttering her odd words, they made their way out of the cottage and remounted their horses. Alyce was subdued on the ride to the castle. The threat to Fredrick had spurred her to action, but now she was wondering if she should have waited for Thomas to return. If Maeve's words were true, she might have two deaths on her conscience after tonight.

"We must try to be sure that no one drinks too much of the drugged ale," she told Fantierre.

"You're worried about the old woman's prediction."

She nodded. "I don't want anyone to die."

Fantierre gave a fleeting smile. "Ah, that is the Saxon heritage in you, *ma belle*. We French are not so ponderous about death. One lives and one dies. It matters little. It's but the start of the next adventure."

Alyce shivered. "It's an adventure that can wait, as far as I'm concerned. In fact," she added ruefully, "after tonight, I'll have had enough of adventure for a very long time."

If Ranulf had not been Thomas's brother, Kenton might have given him a swift punch in the jaw. As it was, all he could do was rail at the slender younger man.

"Would you have had me tie her to a tree to prevent her leaving?" Ranulf asked.

"Exactly!" Kenton roared. "I'd never have left

her in your care if I'd thought you'd be stupid
enough to let her ride away. To Sherborne, no
less." He gave a growl of agony. "Thomas will
have us all cleaning stables for the rest of our lives,
and that's if we get her back safely. If we don't,
we might as well just fall on our swords and have
an end to it."

"The plan has some merit," Ranulf argued.
"Fantierre seemed to think it could work."

"He's French, Ranulf," Kenton said in exasperation, as if that explained everything.

"Will you do as she asked? Can we get the men
ready to ride?"

"We have little choice. My guess is that we'll
get there to find a garrison of fully armed, fully
awake soldiers, but now that Alyce is in their
hands, we have to go in, no matter the conse-
quences."

Ranulf looked sober, as though finally realizing
that the plan Alyce had made sound so logical actually was rather far-fetched. "I'm afraid you're
right, Kenton. I have a feeling that Richard and
John won't be the only brothers at war once
Thomas finds out what I've done."

Kenton was looking off down the road, where a
group of horsemen had just appeared around the
bend. "We'll soon find out, Ranulf, for unless my
eyes deceive me, that's Thomas riding toward us
now."

* * *

Not one part of the plan had gone smoothly, Alyce thought gloomily, as she sat imprisoned in her bedchamber. Fantierre had hoped to be able to buy her some time by declaring that she was his prisoner. But immediately after they'd ridden boldly in through the castle gates, Dunstan's guards had seized *both* her and Fantierre. Her last view of the Frenchman had been of him sending her one of his gallant smiles with a wink as they dragged him across the yard.

She had been able to slip the pouch full of powder to a stable boy, but she had little confidence that the lad had been able to understand her hurried instructions. It was, at least, a slight hope, and kept her from complete despair as she watched the sun setting outside her window. She'd been sent no supper and no drink, so she had no way of knowing if any of the drug had been used.

Her main worry was for Thomas's men. If they stormed the gate after midnight tonight and found the Dunstan men waiting for them, lives could be lost, and more than just the two Maeve had predicted.

Alyce walked over to the window. It was three floors to the courtyard below. She wondered if she could jump to the ground and try to warn Kenton and Ranulf. The area under her window was paved with flagstones. A jump would surely break her legs, if it didn't kill her. She sighed and walked back to the bed. There must be something she could do.

The knock on her door was so soft she hardly heard it. Why was someone knocking, she wondered, when they'd locked her inside? Then the door creaked open.

On the other side was Fredrick. Alyce ran to him with a little cry and threw her arms around him, obviously embarrassing the young man.

"I thought they were holding you prisoner," she told him.

"They were," he said, then he gave an impish smile. "But it appears that Dunstan's guards are very tired tonight."

Alyce's skin prickled with excitement. "They've taken the drug? It's working?"

"Aye. The stable lad took it to the cooks, and they doctored the ale and spread the word among the rest of the household not to drink it. Everyone was in on it. Some of the serving girls took it upon themselves to, ah, make sure that all of Dunstan's men were provided with ample doses."

"Bless them all," Alyce said fervently. "So the hostages are free?"

"Aye, with their guards snoring soundly."

"What about Fantierre?" she asked.

Fredrick's smile died. "I'm sorry, milady."

Alyce clutched his shoulder as a shiver of dread went down her back. "What happened?"

He shook his head. "I'm afraid that Dunstan had

discovered that he was working for Richard. That's why they seized him when he brought you in this afternoon.''

Alyce's throat closed. ''What have they done with him?'' she asked.

''He's dead, milady. I'm sorry. Dunstan had him put to death.''

It didn't seem possible. Gallant Fantierre, who had so carelessly shrugged off danger for all these months. Tears welled in her eyes.

''The next adventure,'' she said, her voice thick.

''Milady?''

She bit her lip. ''That's what he said death would be—like setting off on the next adventure.''

Fredrick's eyes were sympathetic. ''Everyone here liked him.''

She nodded. She couldn't let herself think about Fantierre now. The task was only partly accomplished. Dunstan's men might be asleep, but unless she opened the gates to admit Kenton and the others, they would eventually wake up and take control again.

''What about the baron himself?'' she asked Fredrick. ''Was he given the drugged ale?''

Fredrick shook his head. ''No one knows, milady. He wasn't in the great hall with the rest of his men at supper. We think one of his guards took him some food, but we can't be sure.''

''Well, he's only one man. We won't worry about him. You and I must get to the front gate.

By now Richard's men should be waiting outside.''

Thomas couldn't remember ever having been so angry and so frightened at the same time. He'd ridden back to Sherborne feeling triumphant. Richard's ability to mobilize forces in four parts of the small island country at once had convinced John to talk, and the brothers had worked out an agreement with surprising speed. The king would continue to rule upon his return to the Continent, but if he did muster the troops for another Crusade, he would appoint John as regent while he was in the Holy Lands.

It all seemed to be settled, and Thomas brought papers from Prince John to Dunstan ordering the baron to vacate Sherborne at once. Even though Dunstan was evil and ambitious in his own right, Thomas was convinced that he would not continue to hold Sherborne without the prince's support.

The peace between the royal brothers meant that perhaps he and Alyce could finally have the time to find their own peace. They'd see to it that things were back to normal at Sherborne, and then he'd tell her about Lyonsbridge and take her to meet his grandparents.

But his pleasant daydreams had been shattered the moment he'd dismounted at the campsite outside Sherborne. He could tell immediately from the faces of his brother and lieutenant that something had gone horribly wrong.

Now, as he and his men waited impatiently outside Sherborne Castle, he berated himself again and again for having left Alyce alone. He should have never let her come in the first place, and when he'd had to return to Nottingham, he should have taken her with him.

What a frustrating, obstinate, headstrong, foolish wench she was, he thought. He couldn't imagine life without her.

A full moon had risen in the eastern sky, giving an eerie illumination to the jagged walls of Sherborne Castle. Thomas craned his neck in the vain hope that he might spot her, out walking on the walls or hanging out a tower window. Anything to tell him that she was still alive, still unharmed.

"It's only a few minutes past midnight, Thomas," Ranulf said, riding up beside him. "She said an hour."

Thomas hadn't spoken to Ranulf since Kenton had told him what had transpired. He was so furious with his little brother he was afraid that anything he said would be something he might later regret. But he could tell from the anguished look in his eyes that the young knight was almost as worried as Thomas.

"Aye," he said stiffly. "We'll wait the hour. If the gate's not open by then, we go over the wall."

*   *   *

Alyce looked around her in amazement. Everywhere she turned in the great hall, men wearing the Dunstan livery were stretched out, sound asleep. Some were on the floor, others lay with their heads on the table, next to the flagons of ale that had put them in that state. God bless old Maeve, she prayed silently.

Alfred was waiting for her. He looked none the worse for his ordeal. In fact, there was a bit of fire in his eye and an enthusiasm in his step as he said to her, "Good job, milady. Your father always said that you could outthink ten men, and I have to say he was right."

She embraced him as she had Fredrick. They were her servants, but they were also her family. Everyone at Sherborne was, and they had all worked together to prove it. "I did nothing but bring the powder, Alfred. 'Twas the rest of your staff who made this happen." She gestured to the sleeping men.

His wrinkled face stretched into a broad smile. "Aye, they did," he agreed proudly.

But there was no time to gloat over their triumph. It was past midnight, and she had to get to the front gates, where she fervently hoped Kenton and his men would be waiting.

Leaving Alfred to watch over the sleeping men, she and Fredrick made their way across the bailey. The usual torches along the castle walls had not been lit, but the moon lent plenty of light to their path.

They skirted the small building where Thomas had taken her on his first visit to show her the chests of ransom money. That day seemed years ago, she thought. So much had transpired.

As they came to the end of the stone structure, a shadow stepped out from behind it.

"You're going to pay for this, you witch." The deep, sinister voice was unmistakable. She could see his black eyes in the moonlight. It was Dunstan.

Chapter Seventeen

He lunged at her, and before she could make a move, he'd seized her. Fredrick cried out and drew a dagger from his belt, but by then Dunstan had whirled her around and was holding her with a knife pressed against her neck.

"Drop your knife, villein," he told Fredrick.

The younger man stood, hesitating. Dunstan squeezed his arm more tightly around Alyce, eliciting a groan. Fredrick's knife clattered to the ground.

Dunstan was much bigger than she and his arms were strong. She didn't even attempt to struggle against them. "I would have married you, you piece of baggage," he growled in her ear.

His voice sounded demented, and the brief glimpse she'd had of his eyes had shown her that they looked crazed. She felt a wave of despair. Victory was so close! But now, if Dunstan could succeed in rousing some of his men before she had a chance to admit Kenton and the others, there could still be more bloodshed.

Fredrick was standing in front of them, uncertain. Giving a sudden push backward with all her might, Alyce yelled, "Run, Fredrick! Open the gates!"

Taken off guard, Dunstan momentarily lost his hold on her, but as Fredrick raced away toward the front of the bailey, he grabbed her again with a vicious yank to her hair. "Let them come," he said. "The cause is lost, but, by God, I'll deliver you back to Brand in pieces."

He dragged her to the stables, where a huge black stallion was already saddled and waiting. Lifting her easily, he threw her upside down over the horse's neck, then boosted his tall frame into the saddle behind her.

He must have already learned about the small rear gate, because he steered his horse directly toward it. The door had been closed since Alyce's childhood because it led directly to a precipitous drop into the old castle moat. Looking up from her uncomfortable position over the saddle horn, she was surprised to find the gate standing open. Dunstan had evidently already prepared his getaway.

She held on tightly as Dunstan spurred the stallion forward, heedless of the treacherous terrain on the other side. As soon as the animal passed through the gate, it skidded on the dirt incline and began to stumble. Dunstan pulled firmly on the reins and kept its head upright. Alyce held her position by clinging to the stallion's neck. Horse, rider and passenger slid down the bank into the mostly dried up moat.

When they reached the bottom, the horse lurched, trying to regain its balance, while Dunstan fought to keep from toppling off. Alyce took advantage of the opportunity to push herself away and slide to the ground. She landed on her back with a jarring thud, then rolled quickly away to keep the stallion's hooves from trampling her.

"Come back here!" Dunstan roared, but Alyce was already scrambling back up the bank toward the rear castle door. He tried to rein the horse around in the other direction, but the animal was too frightened from its plunge to follow its master's lead.

A rider thundered around the corner of the wall. Dunstan saw him and, abandoning his pursuit of Alyce, kicked his mount and urged it to climb the opposite bank of the moat. The horse balked for a moment, then, after receiving another vicious kick, started up the incline.

"Hold, Dunstan!" the horseman cried, and Alyce recognized Thomas's voice. She reached the top of the bank and sagged against the open gate, breathing hard.

Dunstan got to the top of the moat just as Thomas, his sword drawn, reached him. "You're not going anywhere, Dunstan," he shouted. "You'll face the king's justice for the murder of Henri Fantierre."

Dunstan raised the hand that held the dagger he'd used against Alyce. Thomas was out of range of his arm, so the baron threw the knife toward his opponent. It hit Thomas a glancing blow on the shoulder, then fell to the ground.

"Surrender, Dunstan," Thomas told him. "I have no problem with killing you, but I'd rather not do it in front of my bride."

Dunstan gave a roar of rage and dug his spurs into the stallion's side. The big animal, already unsettled, staggered, then seemed to teeter on the lip of the moat for an endless moment before it crashed sideways and fell back into the ditch, with Dunstan flailing helplessly on its back. Alyce watched in horror as the big animal smashed to the ground, pinning the baron beneath him.

The night suddenly seemed abnormally quiet for a long moment, then the big stallion gave three sharp snorts and struggled to its feet. Thomas dismounted and slid down the bank to try to pull Dunstan from underneath its big hooves. The panicked stallion took off along the bed of the moat.

Thomas knelt down beside Dunstan, who lay still in the mud. Alyce slipped back down the bank, partly on her feet and partly on her bottom. "Is he hurt?" she asked.

Thomas stood and shielded Dunstan's body

from view. "Don't look. He's dead. Are you all right?"

She nodded, then, ignoring his attempt to protect her sensibilities, stepped around him to look at what was left of Philip of Dunstan.

His body lay partly submerged in a depression in the moat bed that had filled with water from recent rains. She stood looking at it for a long moment. Then she felt Thomas's arms around her shoulders. "It's over," he said. "Let's go."

She shook her head and said, "Thomas, look."

The puddle of water in the moat bed cast back a wavy reflection of the full moon. They watched while the image of the moon turned scarlet as the puddle filled with Dunstan's blood.

"The blood moon," Thomas said.

"Aye."

"He probably wants nothing more to do with me, Lettie," Alyce told her nurse as they sat together polishing silver in the great hall, "and that's fine with me. I'm just happy that everything's back to normal at Sherborne. Thomas can ride off with the king to Normandy for all I care."

It had been a fortnight since Dunstan's death. Lettie had arrived from Nottingham a few days before, her face lined with concern until she saw that her charge was healthy and had come to no harm.

Thomas and his men had stayed only long

enough to be sure that all of Dunstan's troops vacated the premises.

When he rode away with his men, Thomas had been on speaking terms with practically no one. He was still furious with his brother for letting Alyce ride to Sherborne by herself. Kenton was angry with Thomas for refusing to settle things with his brother and Alyce. And Alyce, riddled with guilt about the death of Fantierre, had tried to stay as much as possible out of his way. He hadn't sought her out for a private moment. Their goodbyes had been said in front of all his men and the Sherborne servants.

Once again, she had put his men in danger, and this time it had resulted in the death of a good man and loyal friend. It didn't surprise her that Thomas had left Sherborne as soon as he could, and it wouldn't surprise her if she never saw him again, though the thought seemed intolerable.

"He'll be back," Lettie said.

"I don't think so. Not this time. I think he's washed his hands of me."

Lettie bent over the tray she was polishing, rubbing furiously at a spot of tarnish. "Men are stubborn sometimes, Allie. It's that troublesome pride of theirs. But love usually overcomes it. Love or lust," she added.

"I'll just take Father's advice and live without them."

Lettie set down the tray with a clank. "Alyce

Rose, if I hear that from ye one more time I'm going to take ye over my knee. It would be the first time I've ever done it, but I'm thinking it's not too late."

Alyce was surprised at her vehemence. "You heard my father express those sentiments a hundred times, Lettie. You never seemed to object."

Lettie reached over and took her charge's hand. "Lass, ye were too young to understand, but yer father was a changed man after yer mother died. He never got over her death. They had a true love match, those two."

"I always felt that. In fact it struck me as strange that he was so set against my finding a man when he and my mother had been so happy together."

"They were too happy together. When she died, he nearly went crazy with the grief, and it was worse because he blamed himself."

Alyce sat up straight. "He blamed himself?"

"Aye. She had a lot of trouble birthing ye, and she probably should never have tried to have that second child."

"But my father wanted a son."

"The truth is, he argued against it, but she was always able to talk him into her way of thinking. That's another thing ye inherited from her," Lettie added with a sad smile.

"If she wanted the baby, it was her decision to take the risk of having it," Alyce said, feeling in that moment a perfect kinship with the mother she sometimes could hardly remember.

"That's the logical way to look at it," Lettie agreed, "but yer father never saw it that way. He blamed himself the rest of his life."

"And when anyone asked to court his daughter, he turned them away because it reminded him of his own lost love?"

Lettie was still holding her hand, and gave it a squeeze before letting go. "'Twas more than that. I think he was afraid of losing ye, just like he lost her. Ye're slender like yer mother."

"He was afraid I'd die in childbirth?" The idea seemed ridiculous to Alyce. She'd always been as healthy as a horse.

"I believe he was. If he could convince ye to be happy living out yer life unwed here at Sherborne, ye'd never have to face the risk of having children of yer own. It was wrong of him and selfish."

Alyce sat staring into the shiny silver surface of the bowl she still held. "He thought it was for my good," she said softly.

Lettie sighed. "Aye, I know he did. He was a good man, but he was wrong. For one thing, ye're nothing at all like yer mother. Ye're much stronger than she ever was."

A distorted version of Alyce's face looked back at her from the curved surface of the bowl. Oddly, she looked all at once like the dim memories of her mother that sometimes came to her as she was dozing off to sleep. Her beautiful young mother who had risked everything to bring another child into the world.

Alyce set down the dish and gave herself a little shake. Perhaps her father had been right. She had no fear of childbirth. She was strong, as Lettie had said. But he may have been right that a peaceful life at Sherborne would be for the best. She already had her family here. She could live without children of her own, and she could live without a man who rode in and out of her life as swiftly as a thundercloud.

"I tell you, Thomas, the old woman was a true witch. Never mind the drugs. What about the prophecies?" While Thomas finished writing a letter to give to the courier leaving shortly for Lyonsbridge, Ranulf sat with his feet up on the table. He leaned toward his brother and spoke in an awed voice. "What about the blood moon?"

Thomas gave a snort. Sherborne had been buzzing with the wonder of Maeve's predictions after the death of Dunstan. "It was a puddle of blood, Ranulf. Don't be dramatic."

"And the two deaths? Just like she told Alyce. Dunstan and Fantierre."

Thomas winced. It still caused pain each time he thought about the intrepid Frenchman. "Ranulf, don't you have an appointment with the armorer? I have to finish this.'' He gestured to his letter.

''We should be on our way back to Lyonsbridge rather than sending letters,'' Ranulf grumbled.

''We will be soon, if everything goes as planned.''

''Then you've refused Richard's request to accompany him to the Continent?''

''Aye. I have other plans for my life.''

Ranulf let his feet clunk to the ground. ''I trust those plans include the lady Alyce,'' he said. ''Because, I swear, brother, if you don't want her, I just may—''

''Don't even think it,'' Thomas said firmly.

Ranulf hid a grin. ''Sorry. I didn't mean to make you angry at me again. I reckon I've used up my brotherly forgiveness currency for a spell.''

Thomas looked up and smiled. ''You're a rascal, little brother. And it's hard to stay mad at you.''

Ranulf grinned. ''Lucky for me, since I seem to manage to get myself in the soup with some degree of regularity.''

Still he made no move to leave, but watched quietly while Thomas's quill scratched across the vellum. Finally Thomas looked up and said, '''Tis none of your business.''

''Lyonsbridge is my home, too,'' Ranulf said, a little indignantly. ''If there's news to be told—''

''This has nothing to do with Lyonsbridge. I'm writing to our grandmother Ellen.''

Ranulf's eyebrows went up in surprise. "So what's the great secret?"

Thomas smiled calmly. "I'm asking Grandmother to help me with a financial proposition. As I said before, Ranulf, it's none of your affair."

"I don't know the lady of Lyonsbridge, Fredrick. I'm certain of it," Alyce told her young servant, puzzled. "Where's your grandfather? He would know if my father ever had dealings with Lyonsbridge. It's in the south, isn't it?"

"About halfway between here and London, the lady said."

"And she didn't say what she's doing this far north?"

"All she would say is that her business is with Lady Sherborne and none other. And, milady, she looks to be older than Grandfather." He looked as if such a thing was unthinkable.

"I trust you made no comment in that regard, Fredrick."

"Nay, I wouldn't do that. And, to tell the truth, she's still beautiful in a way. She has these kind of golden eyes and snow-white hair. She looks…regal, I guess ye would say."

Obviously the visitor, whoever she was, had made quite an impression on Fredrick, who usually was far more interested in farming methods than he was in how a person looked.

"You say she's waiting in the solar?" Alyce asked him.

"Aye, milady. Her manservant brought along a trunk. I don't know if they're planning to stay here."

"Of course, we shall offer them hospitality for as long as they wish," Alyce said, but she continued to be mystified. It was so rare that visitors came as far off the main roads as Sherborne, yet in the past year many certainly had.

The woman waiting for her in the sunny room that was Alyce's favorite in the castle was, as Fredrick had said, regal. That was the only way to describe her. Yet for some reason Alyce didn't feel the least bit uncomfortable with her. In fact, she liked the lady Lyonsbridge immediately.

"How kind of you to visit, milady," she told her, making a little curtsy. She was unsure of the woman's rank, but she had the impression Lyonsbridge was a far larger estate than Sherborne, and, in any event, the woman's age merited the deference.

The visitor sat straight on the little bench, the only signs of her age the fine wrinkles of her face and the snow-white hair that Fredrick had noted, which she wore plaited into a kind of crown around her head.

"You must call me Ellen," she said. "And I will call you Alyce, if I may." Her voice, too, sounded surprisingly young.

"I'd be honored," Alyce answered, taking a seat across from the older woman. But the invitation just heightened the mystery. Why had this noblewoman come to Sherborne, and why was she treating Alyce as if they were close friends?

She decided it would be rude to ask the question directly, but she said, "You've had a long day's journey from Lyonsbridge. Are you en route somewhere?"

"Nay, child. I've come just to see you."

Eyes widened, Alyce waited a moment for the woman to continue. When she didn't, Alyce murmured, "Forgive me, Lady…Ellen. I'm afraid if you had business with my father, he never told me anything about it."

"I never had the privilege of knowing your father, Alyce. This is my first visit to Sherborne."

The woman seemed to be studying her, waiting for her to speak, but Alyce was at a loss to explain the strange visit. "Well…we're happy to have you here," she said. "'Tis a modest estate, but I'm very proud of it, and I'd be happy to show you around."

"Another time, perhaps," the older woman said with a gentle smile. "I'm sure you'd rather hear why it is I've suddenly shown up on your doorstep."

With a little sigh of relief, Alyce admitted, "Aye, it has aroused my curiosity."

"I'm an old lady, child," Ellen began, putting

up a hand to ward off Alyce's protest. "I've seen many changes in my time, but one thing that hasn't changed much is that the men in our world still seem to be more in control when it comes to the destiny of us women."

Alyce wondered how much the lady Ellen knew of her story. From her comment, it seemed that she might know quite a bit. "Aye," she agreed mildly. "That has been my experience."

"You, for example, must marry the king's choice. Am I correct?"

Now that her betrothal to Thomas seemed to be meaningless, Alyce was not sure whether King Richard was still going to claim his right to marry her off, but she said, "Aye, by the feudal laws, the king has the right to dictate a husband for me."

"Unless you pay the tax to relieve you of that duty," Ellen added.

Alyce nodded.

"Forgive an old lady her aches and pains, Alyce. It's easier for your young body. Could you please open that chest for me?"

She pointed to a wooden trunk that sat a short distance away. Bewildered, Alyce got up and went to open the trunk. As she did so, her mind flashed back to a similar scene, months ago, when Thomas had also invited her to open a chest. That one had been full of gold coin.

Somehow she knew even before she opened it that this chest would have the same contents. She pushed back the lid and looked over at Ellen, her expression questioning.

"It's a gift," Ellen said. "To pay your tax to the king. There should be enough there to buy your freedom."

Alyce shook her head in confusion. "But why—"

"So you can choose your own destiny, child. We all should have that right."

Alyce looked down at the glittering coins and blinked. It made no sense. Why would a perfect stranger ride into her home and her life and offer her a tremendous amount of money? "I have no land for sale," she said.

The old woman laughed. "I haven't come to buy anything. The money is yours, free and clear."

Alyce sat back and put her hands on her hips. "I don't understand," she said.

Ellen looked at her a long moment, then smiled kindly. "My mission was to bring you the money, child, with no further explanation. But I've had a change of heart."

"I don't understand," Alyce repeated.

"I believe you deserve to know where the money is coming from. It might help you with some decisions you have to make."

"It's not from you?" Alyce asked.

The old woman flashed a grin, and suddenly, in spite of her age, Alyce saw an unmistakable family resemblance. "Nay," Lady Ellen said. "The money is from the heir to Lyonsbridge, my grandson, Thomas Brand."

Chapter Eighteen

Alyce knelt in front of the chest of gold in stunned silence. It was a great deal of money, but probably not much of a consideration to a man who would be heir to the great Lyonsbridge estate.

She could feel heat burning her cheeks as she remembered with embarrassment how she'd thought Thomas was a fortune hunter. She'd thought that his attentions to her were because he had designs on modest little Sherborne. She felt like a fool.

Lady Ellen was waiting for her reaction, but Alyce didn't know what to say to the woman. It was obvious what this meant. After all the trouble she'd caused him, Thomas was no longer interested in marrying her. She supposed the money was in the way of an apology. He didn't want her, but he didn't want her to be forced into any other disagreeable match.

"You can tell your grandson that he has no obligation to me," she said stiffly.

Ellen laughed. "I think he would disagree with you about that."

Tears sprang to Alyce's eyes. Slowly she closed the chest, rose to her feet and went back to sit across from Ellen. She would *not* cry, she told herself fiercely. Thomas was trying to do the decent thing. He wanted to help her find that life of independence she had craved. But evidently he hadn't been willing to see her one last time to bring her the money himself. He'd recruited his grandmother for the task.

"Why did he send you?" she asked Ellen.

"Because I'm a woman, and because I may have some kind of understanding of the feelings of a woman who has had to fight her own battles."

The words sounded more like Ellen's than Thomas's. Alyce had never felt that Thomas had understood much about the kind of battles women had to face. "Or perhaps he was just being cowardly," she said softly.

Ellen chuckled. "Most men are cowards where women's feelings are concerned, but nay. You've taught my grandson a lesson, child. I think this time he wanted to be sure that you felt absolutely free to make your own choice about a husband. He realized it was a mistake to force you before."

"It was," Alyce agreed.

"Mayhap, but I believe it was done with a good

heart. Men always think they know what's best for us.''

"Aye." She thought of her father. He'd felt that he was doing what was best for his daughter by driving away any man who would offer her love. She sighed. "This is generous of Thomas, but you can tell him that he doesn't need to worry about me, and I free him of all obligation.''

Ellen blinked in surprise. "That sounds almost as if you're not in love with him anymore.''

Tears filled her eyes, but her chin went up. "Who said I was ever in love with him? As you must know, King Richard forced me into our betrothal.''

Ellen shook her head. "An old woman knows these things, Alyce. What's more, I don't believe you've stopped loving him. When you said his name just now, I saw the same softness in your eyes that you will see in mine every time you hear me say the name of my husband, Connor.''

She did see it, a mixture of pride and warmth shining from the old woman's still-young eyes. "Aye," Alyce said, her voice subdued. "I do love Thomas. But I'm going to ask you, as one woman to another, to keep my admission a secret. I've caused him a lot of problems and don't blame him for wanting to be free of me. I won't place any more burdens on him.''

Ellen sat straight up in her chair and crossed her

arms. "Blessed St. Mary, child, what makes you think he wants to be free of you?"

Alyce faltered. "Well, it's…it's clear, isn't it?" She gestured toward the money chest. "He's sent me money to pay the king so that I can be free from his choice of a husband. We'll dissolve our betrothal and—"

Ellen leaned forward and seized both of Alyce's hands in a surprisingly strong grip. "Alyce, my child. The last thing Thomas wants is to be free of you. He sent the money so that you could freely choose to marry *him*."

The first sight of Lyonsbridge Castle took Alyce's breath away. She knew it immediately, since Ellen had told her of its distinctive shape, one tower round and one octagonal. The procession rounded a curve and there it was in the distance, silhouetted against the pink sky of the setting sun.

"It's magnificent, isn't it?" Ellen called to her, leaning out from her litter. "I'll never forget my first glimpse of it. 'Twas at sunset, much like today."

"It looks almost golden," Alyce answered, her voice awed.

"Aye. I'll not forget my first glimpse of the master of its stables, either," the old woman added with a chuckle.

Alyce had been amazed to learn that the stable

master she referred to was the same man who was now Ellen's husband, the lord of Lyonsbridge. Of course, Connor's Saxon ancestors had been lords at Lyonsbridge long before Ellen's Norman father had taken possession of the estate.

Alyce had learned a lot about Lyonsbridge history. The previous day at Sherborne, she and Lady Ellen had talked all the afternoon and late into the night.

Ellen had been sympathetic and indignant listening to Alyce's tale of her forced betrothal. For Alyce, it was almost like having a mother to confide in once again.

When Alyce had declared that, in spite of Thomas's gesture with the money, he didn't deserve to have her riding meekly back to Nottingham for a wedding, Ellen had agreed. But as the candles burned low in the cozy solar, the older woman had convinced Alyce to pay a visit to Lyonsbridge.

"It will put you under no obligation, child. I'd like to have you meet Connor and I'd like to show you my home. If my grandson is interested in seeing you, he can come to you there."

So they had set out, Ellen generously sharing her litter with Lettie. Alyce had brought along Fredrick, as well as the two cousins, Hugh and Guelph, since she hadn't wanted to arrive at the great Lyonsbridge unescorted.

In spite of Ellen's show of enthusiasm upon

their arrival, Alyce could see the exhaustion of travel in the woman's face as they made their way up the little hill and through the Lyonsbridge gates. But the weariness seemed to vanish as she turned her head toward the figure of a tall, older man striding toward them across the courtyard.

Connor, Lord of Lyonsbridge, was as snowy-haired as his wife, and his skin showed the same translucence of age. But his back was as straight as a young man's and there was a youthful twinkle in his blue eyes.

He briefly acknowledged Ellen's introduction of the visitor, but Alyce could see that he would pay her little attention until he had first greeted his wife with a tender kiss and asked her, "How did you fare on the journey, my love?" Alyce felt her heart swell a little at the obvious devotion between them.

The evening meal in the huge great hall of Lyonsbridge was merry, and all the Sherborne delegation enjoyed themselves in spite of the fatigue of the journey. Following dinner, Connor picked up his lute, and, his eyes never leaving Ellen, played several minstrel ballads, most dealing with tangled tales of intrigue and love.

Alyce watched him play, her eyes blurry with tears as she recalled how his grandson had sung those very same songs at Sherborne.

Finally, it was obvious that Lady Ellen had reached the end of her strength. She sagged a little in her chair and put her elbows heavily on the table in front of her. Connor set aside his lute and helped her up, stopping only long enough to take leave of his guests before he escorted her out of the room.

Alyce, too, felt the effects of the journey, and was grateful to be shown to a small private chamber that Ellen had ordered prepared for her. Lettie volunteered to sleep on the stone floor beside the single pallet, but Alyce told her to seek more comfortable quarters elsewhere. She was used to sleeping alone, and in fact she welcomed some time to herself to sort through her jumbled thoughts.

She was glad she had come to Lyonsbridge, whether or not Thomas ever showed up. She felt amazingly at home in the roomy castle, in spite of its grandeur. Connor and Ellen both put her at ease. They were a remarkable couple. Alyce lay back on her cot and smiled as she remembered their tenderness with each other. What a gift to be able to live to a happy old age side by side with a partner you loved beyond words. It was a treasure worth more than all the gold in the world, she thought drowsily as she drifted off to sleep.

Somehow, it didn't seem the least bit strange to awaken and find herself in Thomas's arms. Still half-asleep, she gave a contented murmur and snuggled up against his warm chest.

Thomas chuckled. With a start, she realized that she was at Lyonsbridge, and that Thomas was here, naked, and in her bed.

"I've been waiting an hour for you to wake up, sweetheart," he said, kissing her nose. "I rode all night."

She blinked twice. He was smiling down at her, his eyes slightly red from lack of sleep. "What are you doing here?" she asked, still groggy.

He tightened his hold on her. "My grandmother sent word that you might be favorably disposed to seeing me."

She pulled away. "I doubt the lady Ellen would consider this the proper way to hold an audience."

Thomas grinned. "Oh, I don't know. My grandmother's a bold and adventurous lady, rather like someone else I know."

Alyce smiled. "But, Thomas, we need to talk...seriously."

He donned a mock serious expression. "Very well. What would you like to talk about, milady?"

Alyce hesitated. The truth was, she had little desire to talk when she could feel every ridge of his muscles through the thin cloth of her nightdress. "Well, about marriage and things..." Her voice trailed off.

Thomas seemed to sense that her mind was not on the topic. He moved, ever so slightly, so that the fit of their bodies became intimately close. "Marriage, aye, a noble institution," he said with a grin. "My grandparents recommend it."

She brightened. "They're wonderful people, Thomas. I like them so."

"Everyone does," he agreed. "Would that we all could find such happiness."

"Do you think that you and I ever could?" she asked, a bit wistfully.

He kissed her then, deeply and tenderly. When he had finished, he said, "We already have, love, we just have yet to fully admit it. But I'm ready to change that."

"And that's why you sent me the gold?" She wanted to make absolutely certain. "It wasn't to be rid of me?"

He sat almost all the way up, astonished. "To be rid of you!"

"'Tis what I thought, at first. I'd made such a mess of things, caused so many problems." Her lip trembled. "Poor Fantierre…"

Thomas grew sober, then bent to lightly kiss the quivering lip. "Shh, sweetheart. Fantierre was playing a dangerous game and he knew the odds. I believe Dunstan found out about the Frenchman's double role before he ever went to meet with you that afternoon. Your plan to free Sherborne probably had nothing to do with his death."

"But we can't be sure," she said.

"We'll never know," he agreed, "but I do know that Fantierre had a Frenchman's appreciation for true love. The last thing he would want was for his death to spoil things for us."

They both were quiet a long moment, remembering, then Alyce asked the question she'd had ever since Ellen revealed his identity. "Why didn't you ever speak of Lyonsbridge in those days after our betrothal? You were no longer using the Havilland disguise."

"No, but I thought it would be best if I could persuade you to love me for myself, without talk of estates and titles. And when I was asking Lettie about us, she seemed a little insulted at the idea of Sherborne being only a modest holding."

"You've talked to Lettie about this?"

"Sweetheart, I've gotten advice from Lettie and Kenton and Ranulf and my grandmother...even from the king himself." Thomas gave a mock sigh. "I never knew that falling in love was such a complicated subject."

"Nor did I," Alyce agreed fervently. "Of course, it wasn't supposed to happen to me. I was determined to stay unwed."

"Now that would have been a great tragedy," he said, his voice deep with feeling.

She smiled and moved close to him again underneath the blankets. "But I've been convinced to change my mind."

Thomas's slow answering smile set a pulse pounding in the side of her neck. "By my grandmother?" he asked.

"Well, she's been lovely, but...it's been a combination of things."

He pushed her back so that her head was on the

pillow. "Could that saucy Rose have had anything to do with it?"

She wound her arms around his neck. "Aye, I do believe she did," she said with a little giggle. "She's the one who showed me that certain parts of the process can be quite..." she paused as he started to kiss her "...en-joyable."

His tongue stroked from her chin to her lip, then deftly delved into her mouth, seeking a deep, satisfying kiss. "I'll have to thank her someday," he murmured, his voice low and husky.

Alyce gave a little moan and moved to slip her body underneath his. "You can thank her now," she said.

"We have to get up, Thomas. Your grandparents will think me a scandalous hussy."

"I don't think they'll judge us too harshly," he said with a laugh. "I remember many a morning when neither of them showed up to break the fast."

"I have no such memories of my parents," Alyce said, a little sadly. "I think even before my mother died, my father was afraid of what their lovemaking might do to her."

"My grandmother says that to live in fear is to live life as a cripple."

"I can see that spirit in her," Alyce said.

"Of course, from the tales I've heard, there are

times when my grandfather felt that she could have benefited from a little bit of healthy fear.''

"Her way seems to have worked fine for her. She's lived to a healthy old age.''

Thomas rolled over to give Alyce a sound kiss. "You have a lot in common with my grandmother, sweetheart. I may have to ask my grandfather for advice on how to deal with a woman who knows her own mind.''

"I think you've already discovered one way to deal with her,'' she said, kissing him back.

He grinned. "Aye, but I'll continue to ask advice.'' He looked away for a moment, then said casually, "In fact, I was thinking that you and I might pay a visit to old Maeve when we return to Sherborne.''

Alyce was surprised. "I thought you didn't believe in her powers.''

"I've rethought the matter.''

With a sly smile she said, "And I bet I know the prediction you want from her. It's about those dozen children we're supposed to have.''

He looked sheepish. "To tell you the truth, I'd not considered asking her about that.''

"What then?''

He gave a great sigh. "Sweetheart, I'm utterly in love with you, but you must admit you do have a tendency to get into trouble from time to time. I thought old Maeve might be able to give me advance warning so that I'll be prepared the next time my wife decides to, oh, for example, take on an entire garrison of seasoned soldiers.''

She started to give him a playful swat on the arm, but before she could complete the gesture, he seized her wrist, pinned it to the bed and loomed over her. ''Am I to be such a burden?'' she asked, her voice gone husky.

He nodded his head slowly. ''Aye, fearsome. But I'll make the sacrifice.'' Before she could protest, he lowered his head to begin kissing her again. ''As to the matter of those dozen children...''

She returned his kisses for a moment, then, when he didn't finish his statement, pulled away and waited.

''We don't need to talk with old Maeve about that,'' he murmured.

She smiled. ''We don't?''

''Nay.'' He began to nip just underneath her chin. ''We can get started on that all by ourselves.''

''I love you, Thomas Brand,'' she said. Then she let him roll her in his arms as the midmorning sun turned to afternoon.

* * * * *

Discover the joys of
nineteenth-century America with
four brand-new Westerns from
Harlequin Historicals.

On sale July 2000

THE BLUSHING BRIDE
by **Judith Stacy**
(California)

and

JAKE'S ANGEL
by **Nicole Foster**
(New Mexico)

On sale August 2000

THE PAPER MARRIAGE
by **Bronwyn Williams**
(North Carolina)

and

PRAIRIE BRIDE
by **Julianne McLean**
(Kansas)

Harlequin Historicals
The way the past *should* have been.

HARLEQUIN®
*M*akes any time special ™

Take a romp through
Merrie Olde England
with four adventurous tales
from Harlequin Historicals.

In July 2000 look for

MALCOLM'S HONOR
by **Jillian Hart**
(England, 1280s)

LADY OF LYONSBRIDGE
by **Ana Seymour**
(England, 1190s)

In August 2000 look for

THE SEA WITCH
by **Ruth Langan**
(England, 1600s)

PRINCE OF HEARTS
by **Katy Cooper**
(England, 1520s)

**Harlequin Historicals
The way the past *should* have been!**

Romance is just one click away!

online book **serials**

- *Exclusive* to our web site, get caught up in both the daily and weekly online installments of new romance stories.
- Try the Writing Round Robin. Contribute a chapter to a story created by our members. Plus, winners will get prizes.

romantic **travel**

- Want to know where the best place to kiss in New York City is, or which restaurant in Los Angeles is the most romantic? Check out our Romantic Hot Spots for the scoop.
- Share your travel tips and stories with us on the romantic travel message boards.

romantic reading **library**

- Relax as you read our collection of Romantic Poetry.
- Take a peek at the Top 10 Most Romantic Lines!

Visit us online at

www.eHarlequin.com

on Women.com Networks

Dixie Browning
and her sister
Mary Williams
writing as

Bronwyn Williams

are pleased to present their new
Harlequin Historical

The Paper Marriage

Former sea captain Matthew Powers knew he needed
help caring for his newly adopted daughter. A
marriage by proxy to a deserving widow seemed
like a good idea—until his Aunt Bess came to town
with her friend in tow, and he found himself falling
in love with the enchanting Rose.

The latest book in

The Passionate
P**O**WERS
series

Available in August 2000

Harlequin Historicals
The way the past *should* have been!

Available at your favorite retail outlet!

HARLEQUIN®
Makes any time special ™

Visit us at www.eHarlequin.com   HHBWPM